A Single Worry

A Single Worry

by LaJoyce Martin

A Single Worry

by LaJoyce Martin
©1993 Word Aflame Press
Hazelwood, MO 63042-2299
Reprint History: 1996

Cover Design by Tim Agnew
Illustrated by Art Kirchhoff

Printed in United States of America.

Printed by

Library of Congress Cataloging-in-Publication Data

Martin, LaJoyce, 1937–
    A single worry / by LaJoyce Martin.
       p.   cm.
    ISBN 1-56722-011-8 :
    I. Title.
    PS3563.A72486S56 1993
    813'.54--dc20
                                         93-18944
                                           CIP

Dedicated to
Neemommy's Grands:
Cherish, Colton, and Chantél

Contents

CHAPTER ONE

Mama's Worry

Henry Harris always allowed that his wife, Martha, hung her thoughts outside her head to air. "An' it's a good thing, I 'spect," he'd chuckle. "A good breeze blows a lotta wrinkles out."

One week before the Harris reunion, Martha peered over her pince-nez at Sally and said what was on her mind: "I could go to my grave an' kick up gold dust ifn Alan would find hisself a goodly woman an' git married!"

Even before she said it, Sally knew how she felt. Martha's ambition for each of her children had been that he or she find a tailored-to-fit mate. That, in her opinion, was the only way they could be truly happy.

Her wishes started coming true before she was ready. Sarah, her oldest daughter, eloped at sixteen with the neighbor boy, and Henry said Martha cried all night after she found Sarah's note in the sugar bowl. Martha denied it, saying she didn't cry—and that Hank Gibson made such a fetching son-in-law that she forgave Sarah before the week was old.

Another one or two of her brood gave her a season of mental adjusting, but it was like Henry getting his monocle fixed just right—when she got things in focus, she was pleased.

Sally, the youngest of the Harrises, ran away from home when she was eighteen, almost bringing on an apoplexy attack for Martha before she found Jay—or Jay found her. But that was five years ago and seemed another time in another world now.

"Maybe Alan doesn't feel the need for a wife, Mama," Sally suggested.

"A body is just half a body without a helpmeet, Sally." That was one of Martha's favorite axioms. "An' never have I realized it more than since your pa left."

Poor half-Alan, Sally thought, her mind slicing him in two parts horizontally, then vertically to see which looked the worse.

Alan was the only one of the nine Harris children left single. Martha worried about him incessantly. To her, it was as if he had been left out of the Lamb's Book of Life.

"Off in Austin a-solo," she sputtered, hanging out some words that were still hot, "where there's medicine shows 'n dance halls 'n all sorts of bilious devilment! An' exposed to them wicked flappers 'n buzzards of society!"

Sally pictured big birds with women's faces.

"Like a helpless biddy a-swarmed by hawks."

Here Sally's mental photography failed. She could not conjure up a picture of Alan as a baby chicken. No, not Alan.

"Or a—" Martha was getting worked up.

"Alan's big enough to take care of himself, Mama," Sally reminded, trying to calm her down.

10

"Big enough." She gave a sawed-off snort. "But is he *smart* enough? Lot's o' things are big enough, but—"

"He's pretty smart," Sally said. "Smart enough to have a good government job down at the Capitol."

"There's more'n one kind o' smart, Sally-girl." Sally-girl was the pet name Henry gave Sally before she graduated from bloomers. It always reminded Sally of her father when Martha said it that way, and the reminder smarted a little. "There's *book* wise an' there's *spirit* wise. I jest hope Alan has 'um both."

Sally decided to say something she had been wanting to say for a long time. She thought it high time her mother realized it. "Alan is almost thirty years old, Mama, and he's not a child. He is no longer your responsibility."

It was the wrong thing to say. It brought on what Henry used to call "Martha preaching."

"Sally." She looked at her daughter with tired exasperation. "You've never been a mother an' I don't 'spect you to understand a mother's heart until you are one. . . . Do you remember th' day th' twins were born? That was seven years 'fore you came along—"

On days like today, Sally suspected Martha of growing senile before she even reached her promised three-score and ten. At other times, Sally gave her credit for forgetting far more than she had learned in her own twenty-three years.

"—Chester an' Alan looked like a coupla drowned rats when they was born, so tiny an' hairless. What do you call them early babies?"

"Preemies."

"Whatever. Alan was th' smallest of the two. He'd fit into yore papa's hand easy. Couldn't even find his

11

eyebrows er fingernails without a magnifyin' glass! Th' doctor said he was like not to live more'n a few hours, an' Henry didn't go a-fieldin' fer a whole week, just a-settin' and a-waiting' for his last an' final breath. I dare say Parson Stevens was rehearsin' the funeral sermon fast an' furious.

"But he was a fighter, that Alan!" Memory mellowed her eyes.

"Yes, he was a fighter, Mama. I still remember some of the scraps he got into at school. He knocked one of Sonny Grimes's front teeth loose, thinking she was a boy swaggering around in those overalls and cussing and spitting brown—"

Martha effectively ignored Sally. "He surprised 'um all! Th' doctor, th' preacher, an' his own pa. An' just look at him now! Why, he's a good inch taller'n any of th' other boys!"

She tilted her head toward the portrait of Alan in a frock coat. He'd sent it to her for her birthday. "About th' han'somest of all my brood, too. Don't know where he fetched so much han'some. Turns th' heads of ever' girl in th' state o' Texas, I dare say!"

Sally had no argument for that. She could remember from her first primer days how all the upper grade girls would whisper and titter over her big brother Alan. They'd buggy past the Harris homeplace and crane their necks in hopes of a glimpse of him. It rather irked Sally then. She thought girls with nothing better to think about than boys were dumb. She liked cats and wish books and her hoop.

"But jest 'cause he'll soon be turnin' down th' road t' thirty don't turn my heart loose from him," Martha was saying. "Joseph has Amy t' worry over him, William has Nellie, Matthew has Pauline, an' all th' others got worry-partners, too. I thought *ever'body* would be wed by now. But till Alan gets hisself married, somebody's got to worry, an' who's to do it but *me?* I ain't layin' down the woman-responsibility till some helpmeet picks it up. No siree!"

"Look, Mama. He's more than a hundred miles from here, and all your lying awake at night worrying won't—"

"Miles make no matter! Ifn it's a thousand er a million. Thoughts an' prayers can travel any sum o' miles without hooves er wheels er rails."

"I didn't mean quit praying. I meant quit *worrying*."

"Ifn I never worried, I'd likely as not never pray. Worryin' an' prayin' goes hand 'n hand. I don't know ifn that's in th' Good Book, but it might as well be. Prayin's always got a sharer: watchin' an' prayin' er fastin' n' prayin' er *worryin'* n' prayin'. You let *me* worry about my worryin'."

Sally looked into Martha's faded gray eyes—eyes that revealed the strain of piloting many children from cradle to maturity—and tried to put herself into her mother's shoes. Would she bear such burdens twenty, thirty years from now?

The sweep of Sally's glance touched Alan's picture on the wall. His was a face that made a smile feel right at home. His black hair, with one flourish of a wave in the front and the dark eyes that held an essence of humor made him more handsome than any man she had seen in Fort Fisher while on her prodigal journey. She found herself wondering how he had escaped the hooks and lures of romantic anglers—or *angleresses* she supposed the

13

gender would be. His good looks could certainly be disconcerting to any young lady's heart.

Another look at the portrait brought more reflection. Not all her memories were pleasant. When the children were small, Henry seated the family at the long, oilcloth-covered harvest table in chronological order. Although Arthur sat between Alan and Sally, Alan could reach around Arthur to pinch Sally or pull her braids. He constantly teased and was never still. And Sally as consistently sought revenge. His legs grew faster than Martha could keep him in properly fitting britches, and when his shins showed, Sally took the opportunity to kick them. He probably had scars yet.

In boyhood, Alan liked to fish. A lass would have been more apt to snag him on the creek bank than at the city bank, Sally decided. He chased her with worms and whiskered catfish. She hated it—and him. Brothers were an evil necessity for younger sisters. Why was she punished with so many?

But Alan had undergone a metamorphosis. Surprisingly, he had grown up to be a real gentleman with all the South's charm and good manners. He knew how to bow in the middle and tip his hat. He opened doors and pulled out chairs for the ladyfolks. He had gone to school longer than the rest of the children and then gone to the city despite Martha's sputtering. And he hadn't returned as her wishful predictions calculated that he would do.

"He must like city life, Martha," was Henry's only comment. Martha's reaction was a worried look.

Sally went to the city—though not so large a place as where Alan lived—and got her fill of it. Her illusion washed away in mere hours. She got homesick for the country: for the bellowing of the cows, the smell of the freshly plowed garden, the sight of trees with a necklace of hollyhocks in the woods.

"I had so hoped Alan could make it home fer th' reunion this year so's all of us'ns would be t'gether." Martha kept jerking Sally's thoughts back to the present. "But I'm not sure he'll get t' come. He may not can leave his gover'ment job. With important work, you can't jest up an' leave when you're good an' ready. It's not like farmin', where you could put off some o' th' chores fer a few hours if need be. Er do 'um up ahead. I can't imagine Alan likin' anything that ties you down so—"

"He makes good money."

"Filthy lucre." Martha raised her voice. "Is money more important than one's family? Answer me that."

"They have certain days off, Mama. Annual leave, they call it. I'm sure Alan would have reserved some time for an occasion so special as this."

"I've heared from ever' one but him. It jest won't be th' same without *all* my children home."

"I'm sure he'll be here if there's any way he can."

Martha didn't act as if she had heard Sally. Her mind had reverted to its "duty" of worrying. "I sure hope Alan don't up an' choose one o' those spoiled-ritzy-heathen girls with their pretty jest painted on th' outside."

Sally realized that nothing she could say would stanch her mother's fears. Martha was determined to fret over her unmarried son.

She made a quick decision. No matter how many children she had, she would let them go when they were sufficiently grown. She promised herself not to lament if they married or if they didn't. If they did not wish to be "truly happy," that would be their problem, not hers. Why make oneself miserable with something one could do nothing about? No, she'd not let her children affect her the way Alan was affecting Martha. They could live their own lives and make their choices, and she'd live hers. With mental scissors, she cut apron strings before they were even looped and knotted.

Sally yawned. "And suppose Alan never marries, Mama? At his age, I consider that a likely possibility."

"*What?*" Martha bowed her head. "Then I'll go to my grave with no peace o' mind," she said. "I'll never be able t' kick up gold dust—jest *black mud!*"

It seemed settled.

CHAPTER TWO

The Letter

Sally looked up to see Sarah's youngest racing toward the porch where she and Martha sat. The nails of the child's Boston slippers made a rhythmic click on the cobblestone walk.

Matilda was a refreshing youngster too tall for her age, russet haired and green eyed. Her bare legs looked comically long between her short skirt and anklets. Like stilts, Sally thought.

"I jest can't git used t' children without stockin's," Martha complained. "It's a shame, Sally, that th' river o' time has t' erode away our old customs an' eat into our way of life. I'd 'ave never thought of dressin' one of you so scanty as that!"

"I'm glad to see the stockings go, Mama. I hated them. They weren't good for anything but to catch cockleburs and make my legs itchy."

"But it looks so . . . so *immodest*. Especially on a girl a'ready turned seven year old."

"Gra'ma, you got a letter!"

Martha grappled in her apron pocket for her spectacles. "Well, hand it here, Tilly."

Sally had come to expect the certain faraway look in her mother's eyes with each letter that came. That remembering look. It was almost as if time rolled back a generation. Back to when little girls wore long morning gowns and cotton hosiery. Back to "the good old days." Martha would be remembering that time-faded letter that changed her life. Joseph was the one running down the path—a narrow goathead-haunted trail—waving a letter. *Maw, we got a letter . . .*

Sally supposed that Martha had never gotten a letter since without thinking of that life-changing message. She'd heard her mother tell about it time and again— how the letter announced the coming of Papa's niece, Effie, a child twisted in body but pure of mind and soul.

Now Martha frowned. Sally could follow the trail of the story going over the map of her mind by her facial expressions. Martha didn't like some of the memories. They pricked. She hadn't been kind to little Effie; she had even mistreated her, feeling sure that the child's birth defects labeled her a product of sin. Effie's mother must have been "a bad woman," and she was "cursed" with a defective child. But when Effie risked her own life to save Sally from a fire, Martha saw how wrong she had been. Martha tried to make it up to Effie but never felt that she quite succeeded.

When Effie died, her inheritance salvaged the Harris family from bankruptcy and left them well fixed. She was the benefactress of the spacious home place, the talking machine, the porch swing on which they now sat. . . .

Martha said if she could "go backerds," she'd change

some things. But convinced that she couldn't, she rather liked most of life's update. Especially her modern home. She said it was "a fer piece" ahead of the "lopsided shack that looked like a woodpile that fell an' sprawled" which once housed them all. Sally was so young, she deemed her recollections of the old place mere mental pictures scribbled on the walls of her memory by the older children's description of it.

If she could collect from yesteryear, Martha said, she'd call back her patient and faithful husband, Henry. It seemed to Sally that Martha almost blamed him for the abrupt way he left her without warning. As if he could help it! The doctor said his "ticker just played out." One of the boys found him dead in the field.

All of the children thought Martha would go first. She had survived a stroke that left one leg dragging a bit, but here she was approaching seventy—and Henry didn't even make his quota of years. Martha laid him beside Robert, the little boy who was killed in a horse accident. Sally didn't remember that either, since Robert met his death before she was born.

Martha grieved for Henry. She didn't think she could go on living without him. Strong and stable, he was her anchor in every storm. But with Sarah living just down the road and Sally and Jay right on the property, it wasn't as though she was all alone. One or another of the grandchildren stayed with her most nights. And Sister Myrt, a neighbor who had been widowed for half a century, visited too often.

After a while, the children persuaded their mother that life has no reverse gears and that she had to go on. She had been "going on" for four years now, and it surprised them all how fast time had passed since they lost their beloved protector and father.

Matilda laid the letter on Martha's lap. "Gra'ma, who is it from?"

Martha adjusted the glasses on the bridge of her nose. "Patience, pet. We'll see. Aren't your legs cold?"

"Nary a bit, Gra'ma. They're plumb warm. Why, it's spring. Hadn't you noticed?"

Martha tamped the envelope, sending its contents sledding to one end, then tore open the opposite side with a quick, jagged rip. "It ain't backed with no return name, but it looks suspiciouslike one o' my boy's handwritin'." She unfolded the single page.

"Which one, Gra'ma?"

Martha glanced at the bottom. "I could most nigh tell without a-lookin'. See how th' letters march acrost th' page with straight backs like soldiers all in rank an' row? Alan signatures it. I knew 'fore I looked."

Matilda clapped her hands. "Uncle Alan! Is he coming for the reunion?"

"Lord's sakes, child! Gimme time. I ain't a fast reader. You rush me up like Joseph used to when I got a letter!"

The child drew a deep breath then let it out slowly. "I'll be glad when I can read for myself."

Martha ignored her pout. "Lemme see here now. He sends greetin's to all. Hopin' we're all doin' well. Hopin' we're not a-workin' too hard. Hopin' th' fish is a-bitin'. He sends a special hello to you, Sally."

Sally nodded.

Matilda fidgeted. "Is that all?"

"No."

"What else?"

"Mind your manners, Tilly," Sally scolded. "It's a message to your grandmother."

"Sometimes my manners just *won't* mind, Aunt Sally. 'Specially when my thoughts are in a hurry to see what's coming next."

Sally laughed to cover her own impatience.

Martha gave a cry of delight. "He can come, pet! He's a-comin', Sally! He will be here for th' reunion!" She raised the note sheet in a flap of victory.

"Uncle Alan's coming? For really?" The girl pirouetted about, her heels drumming a staccato on the porch floor, her petticoats billowing.

"His train'll be arrivin' a-Friday o' this week."

"Will Uncle Alan bring me hoarhound candy again?"

"Likely. He's always been thoughty."

"Ma said Uncle Alan's nigh on to being a batcher."

"A what?"

"A batcher."

"She probably means a bachelor," Sally said.

"What is that?" the child asked.

"It's a man who's old enough t' git married but never got hisself a wife," Martha supplied. "None o' us want Alan to be an old bach'lor. I'm prayin' day an' night he won't be so."

"You mean you *want* Uncle Alan to get married, Gra'ma?"

" 'Course, child. I want another daughter-in-law." She chucked Matilda under the chin. "An' I want more grandchildren jest like you."

"But I rather like Uncle Alan just like he is." The pout came again. "I think he's nice."

"But ifn he marries hisself a nice woman, he'll be *twice*

as nice. An unmarried body is jest half a body."

"Are you just half a body without Gran'pa?"

"Lesser'n that, pet. He was th' biggest an' best half o' my life. But I'm too old an' wrinkled to look fer a new half now. I'll just wait an' join my old half in yon cemetery."

"I do hope Uncle Alan gets a good half," worried the girl.

"Sally an' me was talkin' about that very thing yesterday. In big cities, there's lots of women prowlin' 'round tryin' to find a half better'n theirselves. It would be nice ifn he could find somebody closer to home an' more his kind."

Clasping her hands together, Matilda rolled her eyes upward. "I know who I'd pick for my uncle's other half if I was doing the picking!"

"It'd have t' be somebody special."

"There's only one somebody special in the whole world that would be *delicious* enough for my Uncle Alan."

"An' who might that be?"

"My schoolmarm. Miss Young. She'd be just *perfect* for him, Gra'ma."

"Elise Young." Martha's gray eyes took on a new light. "Jest this mornin' I cooped up that'n in my thinkin' cap. Well, well—out o' th' mouth o' babes . . . What do you think about that, Sally-girl?"

"About what, Mama?"

" 'Bout Miss Young an' Alan matched up."

"I hadn't paired the two together in my mind. Elise is demure and ladylike with a soft spirit. Alan is strong and good-natured. Yes, I think I'd vote for it," she said.

"That's three votes!" counted Matilda, holding up three fingers.

"Why don't you an' me help it happen, Sally?" Martha grew excited with the newborn thought. "We can work real hard t' get 'um t'gether while he's home fer this reunion. He couldn't help hisself from likin' her if he knowed her."

"What harm could be done?" Sally bunched her shoulders.

"And I'll help, too, Gra'ma," Matilda volunteered.

"No! No!" Martha threw up both hands. "Children are t' be seen an' not heard. Oh, this modern generation! Tilly, you're not to say one word. Do you understand? Leave th' match striking to th' adults who can do it an' it not be noticeable."

"Children don't fool with matches," Sally put in dryly.

"We can't afford t' let Alan know what we're about. He might turn jest th' opposite ifn he catches on. I'm thinkin' him girl-shy. An' a man likes t' think he's pickin' his own besides."

"I can't even *whisper* his name to my teacher?"

"Absolutely not!"

"Fiddlesticks!"

"And you must not tell any of your cousins who come to the reunion about the secret." Sally tried to sound stern. "We don't want anything to spoil our plans. The word is mum."

"Will my mother know?"

"Mayhap."

"Aunt Dessie, too?"

"We'll see how much help we need. Too many cooks spoil th' soup."

"How will Uncle Alan and Miss Young meet each other?"

23

"We'll hatch up somethin'." Martha stuffed the letter into her pocket along with her glasses. "With our heads workin' t'gether, we ought t' find some way t' do it so sly-like neither'll know they're bit till it's too late an' they're a'ready infected." She gave a coltish giggle. "Right, Sally-girl?"

"Yes, Mama." Whatever pleased Martha made Sally happy, too.

"But what if Uncle Alan doesn't want to get married at all?"

Sally was trying to think of something to squelch her niece's arguments when Martha spoke up. "Of course he does, pet. All men want t' get married. Some of 'em are jest slow findin' out they want a wife. Think of th' poor, poor darlin' havin' t' live out his whole lifetime in a stuffy boardin'house, payin' a maid t' do his warshin' an' darn his socks an' turn his collars, an' havin' to eat store-boughten bread! An' no one to tend him when he's ailin'." Martha let up long enough to wipe away a real tear. "Why, marryin' was thought up by God Hisself. Th' Bible allows it's good an' honorable. A wife's a heaven's blessin'. He that findeth a wife findeth a good thing. An' ever' mother wants her son to have what's best fer him."

"I wish I was grown up," fussed Matilda. "Grownups have all the fun!"

"Now that's strange, pet. I onct heard yore gran'pa say he wisht he was a child 'cause children have all th' fun."

"I never get to do anything."

"You got to bring me this wonderful letter. An' it's th' best thing that's happened all day."

Somewhat mollified, Matilda ran home to take the news to her mother.

24

Sally looked up at Martha to find a dreamy smile on her face. The worry lines had melted away, and she seemed somehow younger. Sally decided that her mother was seeing what she wished as though it was. It was something the parson called faith.

Sally wished the dream, whatever it was, might last forever.

CHAPTER THREE

Plans

Three blocks from the capitol building in Austin, squeezed between a clothier and a law office, thrived a small cafe.

The eatery was a low-beamed, cellar affair with the menu chalked in on a slate that hung on the wall. But it had a good roasting spit, was clean, and gave good service. Affluent people, as well as commoners, patronized the place.

Helen Jorgensen, daughter of a wealthy Texas politician, often met her friend Claire in the restaurant for lunch. It provided a quiet spot for gossip and girl talk. Today she had something special to share with Claire.

"You've a secret, and you're nearly exploding with it. I can see it in your eyes," teased Claire innocently enough, tucking her parasol under the table. "Out with it."

"Last evening I met the man I'm going to marry." The announcement took no detours.

"You *what?*"

"You heard exactly what you thought you did. His name is Alan Harris, and he has been working with Father on some public school reforms. He's especially interested in seeing that rural communities have equal opportunities for education. He wants trained teachers for all country schools." Her sapphire eyes grew dreamy. "He's the perfect specimen of manhood, Claire."

"If I make no mistake, that's what you said about Ben Prichard."

"No, no, there's no comparison. This is the real thing."

"So you finally found Mr. Right?"

"Yes. He came to the house last night to bring Father some papers. I invited him to stay for tea. I was smitten!"

"Was *he*?"

"I plan to smite him. I invited him back, but he's leaving town—"

"Not for good, I should hope."

"Oh, no. He's taking his annual leave to visit his family and attend to some personal business."

"What did you learn of him? Of his background?"

"One doesn't ask to see all the apples on the family tree or request a genealogical summary at first meeting."

"Helen, you know what I mean!"

"I did learn that he is from a large, close-knit country family. I found him quite easy to converse with and very warm. He answered my questions cordially. His company was a sublime pleasure!"

"He's from a large family, and you're an only child. He's from the country, and you from the city—"

"It's a counterbalance, don't you see? I've always hated being an only child, and my method of compensating for that fact will be to marry into a family such as Alan's. He said his big family was 'more fun than a rain barrel full of wiggletails.' His exact words. I can hardly wait to meet them.''

"What are his hobbies? Does he like to dance? Play polo? Tennis?''

"He likes to hunt and fish.''

"Yuck. How boring.''

"I don't find that so distasteful. Some ships are quite modern nowadays. Even luxurious. One of the old swells in Mum's bridge club has just returned from a cruise. She said the cabins were elegant. Do you know deep-sea fishing is popular now? The mode. And big game hunts are status quo. Especially overseas. A safari sort of thing. Africa. Or in the Amazon tropics. Not that I'd want to honeymoon there, but—''

"Honeymoon? Helen, you are beside yourself. You've only but met the man!''

"Like I said, Claire, I plan to marry him, and Father will send us wherever we wish to go.''

"What does this Greek god look like?''

"Just that. Tall. Dark. Handsome. The whole nine yards. He says he has an identical twin brother—''

"He does?''

"Hold your hatpin, Claire. His brother is married.''

"Rotten luck!''

"Alan is the only single one left in his family. His father is deceased, and I got the impression that his mother is well fixed financially.''

"Well, Helen, if that's who you want, I hope you snag him. But then, I've never seen a man you couldn't snag.''

"Yes, I'm afraid I'm spoiled to getting what I go after.

And this is the only man I've ever wanted to spend the rest of my life with. I have some clever plans to land him in my net when he gets back from his vacation."

"Tell me more, Helen. Any man who could throw *you* head over heels is worth our full hour."

A lone woman took the booth across from them, but they paid her no heed.

"He's older than any other suitors, which gives him a maturity that adds to his other charms."

"Do you know his age?"

"Father says he's twenty-nine."

"Twenty-nine? And still single? How do you account for his escaping Cupid's traps all these years?"

"He hasn't been around much. After his lengthy education, he had to get himself established with the government. He says he has little social life."

"What does your mother think of him?"

"Oh, you know Mother! She'd find something wrong with Archangel Michael: wings too short, nose too long . . . ." She made a face while Claire tried to keep hers straight. "Alan has a childhood dialect to which he sometimes reverts. Mother can't *stand* it! I think it's simply *charming*."

"He hasn't been to any of our parties?"

"He doesn't go anywhere except to church on weekends—and a midweek service, too, I believe he said. Some small church. He gave me the address, even invited me to attend."

"Oh, a religious zealot."

"I could change that. He simply needs something else to think about. Me, for instance."

"Mrs. Alan Harris. That somehow fits you, Helen."

"It looks pretty written down, too."

The young lady at the next table laid aside her napkin and leaned their direction. "Excuse me," she said, raising her too-arched brows a notch higher, "did I hear you speak of Alan Harris?"

Claire waited for Helen to answer, Helen for Claire.

The speaker's painted lips parted in an almost condescending smile. "If we're talking about the same Alan Harris, he is a very close friend of mine."

"I'm sure we are not speaking of the same person." Claire's tone sprinkled ice toward the woman across the aisle, whom she demoted in her mind to several notches below herself on the social scale.

"I had lost track of him since he left home," she continued, unabashed. "He and his twin brother, Chester, once ran a contest of how best to torment me. They used frogs and lizards and worms. And even a snake."

Claire gave a visible shudder.

A greenish cast claimed Helen's face as she reached for her water glass. "A twin?"

"Funny thing about their names," the young woman rambled on. "They were born back when Mr. Chester Alan Arthur was president. He was their mother's political idol. She named the twins Chester and Alan and a year later produced another son whom she named Arthur. She called them the President's boys. There was a whole passel of those Harris kids."

"So you know Mr. Harris considerably well?" Claire found her voice, then wondered if it was really hers as it warbled out.

"Too well, I'm afraid. My grandmother lives in the same settlement as the Harris family. I spent a great deal of my life there. It's a primitive huddle of farms along the Brazos River—a place called Brazos Point. It could hardly be called a town. It's filled with old ladies and their fancywork. Young people leave as soon as possible. Now *Austin*—Austin is a *town*."

"Then maybe you can tell us something about Mr. Harris's upbringing. This is Representative Jorgensen's daughter, Helen, and she is interested in marrying Mr. Harris. I'm Claire."

Helen blushed.

"I can tell you anything you wish to know about Alan Harris. I'm amazed to know that he's here in Austin and I haven't bumped into him yet. I've been to most of the places where singles meet."

"Mr. Harris works with Helen's father at the capitol building," Claire inclined her head to the west. "He's been working there for some time. He's interested in rural schools, mapping out some school reforms and—"

Helen kicked Claire under the table.

"—and please tell us what you know about him and his family."

"I'd be glad to quench your wonder, but I'm afraid there isn't much in his humble beginnings that would interest either of you. What would you like to know?"

Claire looked at Helen. "Well?"

"Would . . . would you happen to know something of their social status and their financial influence in their community? Their political views? All this would be particularly important to my mother. Well bred, well wed, she says."

The woman laughed, but it wasn't a pretty laugh. "The Harrises are as country as cornpone in a black iron skillet, Miss Jorgensen. Backwoodsy, if you please. Alan's mother couldn't even read or write until she was a grown woman! She still has a very poor command of the English language."

"They were immigrants?"

"No, they were hillbillies. Plain ignorant. But Mrs. Harris did see that most of her brood of nine children got a fair education one way or another. They took their lunches to school in *syrup buckets.*" It seemed that the informer drew some perverse pleasure in Helen's discomfort while she talked. "Now you know why Alan is interested in *rural* schools. His nieces and nephews attend the same one-room school he did."

"His family is . . . poor then?"

"Oh, no! They're in high cotton now. A two-story house with a fancy balustrade. A foster child stayed with them, and they got all her money. Alan went to college on part of the crippled child's funds. Then they sent the child away."

Helen had heard all she wanted to hear. "And how long have you lived here, Miss—?"

"Rushing. Molly Rushing. I've been here for about a year. And to think that I haven't crossed paths with dear old Alan even once! I'll have to look him up. He'll be glad to see some homefolk. My! But he must get lonesome with nobody his kind to keep him company. I'll have to see to that, won't I?"

"Don't waste your worry on Alan, Miss Rushing! He's refined! To the city born!" defended Helen. "He isn't at all as you remember him. I do so admire a man who can lift himself from obscurity to the pinnacle of success as he has done! He'll fit right in at the grand governor's ball, to which he will most certainly get an invitation. I can just see him on the marble dance floor, feel his arm around my waist. I can't imagine him wed to a frumpy girl in a calico apron, her hair tied back with a dirty ribbon." Her shortly cropped hair got a flippant toss. "Not Mr. Harris. I can't let that happen to him. I *won't* let it happen."

"He doesn't dance, and he'll never marry anybody outside his religion, Miss Jorgensen. It's forbidden. I know. I go to the same kind of church he does." She glanced down at her stained fingernails and quickly tried to hide them. "That is, you might say, I'm a stray sheep."

"Religion won't be a problem," Helen said. "My mother and father differ on religious views."

"It was my good luck to have met you girls." Molly had hardly touched her food, but she stood to go. "I think I'll walk over to the capitol and give Alan my regards—"

"I'm sorry, but he is not in today, Miss Rushing." Helen's cold tone matched her eyes. "He is, in fact, preparing to leave town on the train tomorrow for a visit to his mother. I'm afraid you'll have to wait until his return to see him."

"Thank you." Molly Rushing pushed past them and out the door without looking back.

"Well, what do you make of that?" Claire asked when she was gone.

"Jealous." Helen curled her lip. "A jealous little demon. Probably someone he spurned years ago. Her motives are as black as her hair. I don't believe a word she said. She was trying to throw me off track; it showed in every word she spoke."

"It's quite evident she knows him."

"Surely. But I dare say his family wouldn't even associate with her because of her low social class, and she is both angry and vindictive."

"She's not bad looking. In fact, she has a 'come hither' demeanor about her that I would consider dangerous."

"She isn't worth a footnote in a library book, Claire. Alan won't give her the time of day. Had he wanted her, he would have kept up with her. Anyhow, I plan to keep him busy until our wedding. . . ."

But Molly Rushing left with plans of her own. She would have to hurry, but she planned to be on the westbound train with Alan Harris when he headed for Brazos Point tomorrow. A visit to her grandmother was long overdue.

Alan, six years older than she, left for higher schooling while she was yet an unfinished woman. At thirteen, she must have seemed to be a silly schoolgirl to the near adult. In childhood, six years could make a generation of difference. He had moved on in life before she had a chance to impress him. Now it would be different.

Still lodged in Molly's memory were Alan's dashing good looks. Why, every girl in the school would have given her silver shoespoon for his attention! And she had just met a snob of a socialite determined to get her claws in him. Ha! She'd show them all!

She would have hours on the train to win him over. And win him she must, for if she waited until she arrived at Brazos Point to start her campaign, she would have a fight on her hands. Martha Harris had never cottoned to her and certainly would do anything to keep her and Alan apart. But Alan had been away from his mother's influence so long that he would now be a worldly-wise master of his own destiny.

Molly had made her mistakes, she admitted to herself, but remorse was not in the fiber of her character. There was the unfortunate marriage to Eli Adams, the roving telephone lineman. Falling for his fast and reckless spirit, she had graduated from "hello" to "I do" in one week. That was because Jay Walls, whom Martha Harris was "saving" for Sally, stood her up at the last minute. She had a score to settle with Martha Harris, and it might as well be settled now. And the pawn would be her beloved son.

Her marriage to Eli hadn't lasted a month before serious trouble developed. When he spent his leisure hours, as well as his paycheck, at a taproom somewhere, Molly retaliated by working as a soda jerk where flirting opportunities flourished. Molly never lacked for male attention, such as it was.

So much of Molly's time in her youth had been blotted up with the second hand life in novels that she could not sort reality from fantasy. Wifely virtues were neither learned nor practiced.

Eli's appearances at home grew farther and farther apart until he didn't come home at all. She supposed he simply moved on without her. Nor did she give the separation a care. She had married him for the good money and good times he promised her, and she had seen neither.

When all of her resources were gone, she wandered about from place to place until she found a night job in Austin. It wasn't a job her grandmother would have approved of.

Granny Myrt probably wondered what had become of her, and until now the woman scarcely crossed her mind. She loathed her granny's hidebound religious ideas.

On numerous occasions, the pious lady had tried to impose them on a rebellious Molly.

But now it was time that she make a visit to Brazos Point. She would embroider a plausible story about her husband being killed. *And who knows? He might be dead,* she informed her conscience. *With such a high risk job, accidents waited in anticipation.*

Martha Harris knew about her wedding and had even attended it. Molly's past would have to be laundered.

It would be easy. Over the years, Myrt had fed on her granddaughter's falsehoods, seldom tasting the truth. Molly would toss out the lie about her husband's misfortune, and her fable would be sure to spread like sunrise just where she wanted it to.

CHAPTER FOUR

Reflections

Alan couldn't sleep. Prospects of a visit to his child-hood home caused his thoughts to churn and tumble and thrash about.

The quietness of the farm would be a welcome respite for his city-battered spirit. Some people thrived on the whir and buzz of city life: the frenzied activities, social events, eating and drinking, playing and partying. Most of his co-workers even liked the business antonyms. Buy-ing and selling. Wrecking and building. Coming and going.

But he could never jell into their "Noah's day" mold. He tolerated the soul-bruising atmosphere only because he felt this is where God had directed him. He couldn't say that he enjoyed his job here, but he had a purpose, a mission: to see that the laws worked impartially for everyone.

For years, his mother connected any government job with war. He had finally convinced her that he chose this vocation to work for peace. He wanted an honest system because truth set people free.

His mind, sometimes going backward, sometimes forward, hopscotched from one segment of his life to another, defying chronology and conglomerating events. He read the book of his history from whatever page the volume happened to fall open.

The revival. He was still in knickers when the brush arbor meeting came to Brazos Point. The traveling preacher, a straightforward man from Louisiana, drew such vivid pictures of sin and hell that Alan imagined his soul soiled with great black spots, plunging toward a pit of boiling fire. The lie he told Mama about the candy he had stolen . . . the time he cheated on a spelling test . . . the bad word he said when he lost his favorite lure. . . . Filled with remorse, he wrestled a chilling fear that he might die that very night.

When the invitation was given, he slid on his knees in the sawdust to the mourner's bench, trying to get there as fast as he could. The journey from the split-log bench to the altar stretched a mile.

Effie. The crippled cousin who lived with them had been gone for a long time now, but her influence would never die. Her forgiving spirit impressed Alan the most. At a young age, he stood outside the woodshed and listened to her garbled prayers after she had been mistreated. He had seen her come out with her crooked smile adorning her glowing face. Whatever she had inside, he wanted.

His family. They had all made good lives for themselves. Papa had been proud of them. Now they were all married but himself, and they had all made good choices except . . .

He'd only met Chester's wife once. Chester married

the year Papa died. Papa had said to give his wife time and she would adjust. But time hadn't handed out any changes from her direction. Alan's spirit ached when he thought of Chester, but he couldn't decide why. Chester had surprised them all—the outdoor boy who went to Fort Worth to lay brick for the pavement. Now, since his marriage, he was training to be a doctor. His wife . . .

With his blanket tossed into a terrible disorder, Alan slipped into sleep's twilight. The moon, high and alone, poured her light upon the angled masses of buildings nearby. And time, driven by a passion to reach infinity, pushed on through the night.

Alan overslept. He knew it was a good thing he'd packed his bags ahead of time. With but minutes left to dress—and none left for breakfast—he grabbed his portmanteau and dashed to the depot where the train hissed impatiently.

"Ticket, please."

Alan pushed his ticket into the outstretched hand and turned to hurry on.

"Walnut Springs, is it?" the conductor smiled.

"Yes, sir."

"Isn't that where they've just built the railroad shops?"

"It is. And a new cotton gin, too. The little town is on a boom. Some predict it'll be running a population to compete with Fort Worth and Dallas before long. Perfect location, good water."

"Going there for work?"

"No, sir. I have a good job here in Austin at the capitol. My mother lives near the Springs, and I'm taking off a few days to visit. A family reunion."

"I see." He was a talkative sort. "Leave your wife behind or send her ahead?"

"I'm not married, sir."

The porter stepped aside as a breathless young woman pushed her way through the door to the day coach.

"May I take this coach, please?" Alan didn't know whether the question was directed to himself or to the man who collected tickets.

"Take whatever car you please, ma'am," the conductor said. "There are no assigned seats. And none reserved today. May I see your ticket?"

The man looked down then up again. "I see that your destination is Walnut Springs, too. All the world must be going to Walnut Springs today."

"*Too?*"

"The gentleman here is disembarking there."

"Oh, how nice."

She waited for Alan to be seated, then took the seat beside him, although there were plenty of vacant seats scattered about through the coach. "I'm ever so glad to have company," she said. "Trains are so boring, and we've three hours—not counting broken rails and washed-out bridges."

In one compact glance, Alan judged the woman to be an experienced traveler. The hat she wore—if it could be called such—tilted so far to one side that he feared it would fall off and land on his person somewhere. What should he do if the unthinkable thing happened?

Her hair, cropped short, almost fell into her eyes like a glossy black waterfall cascading over her forehead, the flow of which had been stopped abruptly with shears. Her lips were too full, the obvious work of much paint. But for her sooty charcoal eyelids, her violet eyes would have been striking. Would he ever get accustomed to the new, liberated look? The movie houses had given women these styles and ideas.

Short hair and much face color must be the latest of fashion. Miss Jorgensen's tresses were short; he'd noticed that the night he called on the representative. Somehow the transformation never failed to shock him, and he was glad his mother and sisters had never taken the scissors to their "glory." The look made modern women appear looser and more worldly. Of course, he reminded himself, he would be considered "old-fashioned" if his views were known.

The woman beside him arranged her handbag, fluffed her petticoats, and then took time to consult her mirror. Embarrassed, Alan looked out the window to grant the woman more privacy for her personal toilet. Quite possibly she had left in a hurry as he did, and he understood that ladies took more grooming than men.

She certainly wasn't a bad-looking girl. She might even be quite lovely if one got to know her. His mother had always said not to judge any person too soon or too harshly.

CHAPTER FIVE

The Trip

The iron monster heaved and coughed, spitting fire
and black smoke. Then it gave an impulsive jerk that
passed from car to car while the slowly moving wheels
complained loudly and the cross ties took up their
monotonous groan. At last they were moving toward
Walnut Springs.

Outside, man's idea of progress tarnished the land-
scape: manmade roads, telephone lines, giant generators
. . . It made one feel proud yet somehow sad. If only
civilization could advance without sacrificing its simplicity!

"Have you relatives in Walnut Springs, sir?" Molly
touched Alan's arm.

Alan jumped. "Ma'am?"

"Oh, I'm sorry to startle you."

"I was just—thinking."

"Please forgive me for interrupting your thoughts."
Her voice was low, modulated.

Alan smiled. "Sometimes I think that I think too
much. I was lamenting what we've lost in the name of

progress." He swept his hand toward the world on the other side of the window.

"But, sir, when we give up one thing we always get something better in return!"

"I like your philosophy. Now what was your question?"

"I said, have you kinfolks in the Springs?"

"No, ma'am, not in the city itself."

"Nearby, perhaps?"

"Yes. My mother lives in a small place called Brazos Point."

"Brazos Point!" Her wide eyes gave the effect of delighted surprise. "Why, I thought I knew who you are! You're one of those handsome Harris boys, aren't you?"

"I'm a Harris. But not the handsome one. That's my twin."

"I knew it! I'm Molly Rushing."

"Molly . . . Molly . . ."

"But surely you remember me! I've seen you at Brother Steven's church."

"It's probably Chester, my twin brother, that you have in mind. We look somewhat alike. He stayed around the home area longer than I. I've been gone for several years. I went off to school."

"I remember both of you. And there was a boy just younger."

"Arthur."

"The president's boys! The three of you were named for President Chester Alan Arthur. Now I have you placed. And you'll remember me when I tell you who I am."

"I hope I shall."

"I am Sister Myrt's granddaughter. She was the church organist for a good century—"

Alan laughed, a rich, full baritone sound. "Everybody remembers Granny Myrt. And fondly, I might add."

"She got as arthritic as the old pedal organ itself, and they had to get a replacement for her. She was in danger of falling apart with the instrument. The last time I visited, they were considering a piano—"

"Yes, they have a piano now. And I miss the organ's mellow, worshipful tone. The sound put me to sleep many a time. I'm afraid there's another victim of modernization."

"What I recall most is the squeaky three-legged stool. I tried to get Granny to quit playing years ago. But if you'll remember, she was lividly jealous of her position."

Alan remembered. She hovered over her music—though she couldn't read a note of it—like a brood hen. When Pauline, the preacher's daughter, learned to play, Myrt came to church a half hour early to stake claim on the spiral, claw-footed stool. "I do recollect that she was very faithful," is all Alan said.

"Your sister Sally and I were in the same class at school. I was acquainted with Sally's husband, too. In fact, I courted him before she did. I worked awhile at the soda fountain in the Springs."

"I apologize that my memory doesn't hold any of that. I'm seven years older than Sally. I must have left for school while you were still quite young."

Dimples made Molly's smile courtly. "It might be to my advantage that you *don't* remember me any better than you do!"

"You weren't that bad?"

47

"Just painfully immature."

"We can all thank God that immaturity isn't a permanent illness. Do you remember the brush arbor revival the summer Evangelist Parsons came from Louisiana?" Alan stopped. "No, you wouldn't. You would only have been three or four years old if you're Sally's age. I was saved in that revival."

"That's the meeting Granny talked about for years. I can only regret that I wasn't older." She changed the subject. "So you'll be in Brazos Point for a while?"

"Not for long, I'm afraid. I've taken a few days of vacation from my job. My family is having a reunion. The once-a-year thing. My mother likes for all her children to be there."

"How charming. Where do you work in Austin?"

"I work for the state. The Department of Education. Next to religion, education is the most important thing we can offer our future generations, Miss Rushing. My parents never had a chance to learn because they lived in a rural area where there was no school. I want my nieces and nephews—and my children and grandchildren —to have a better life with broader opportunities."

"Just call me Molly if you'd like; I consider us friends. And I agree with you wholeheartedly, Alan. I'm delighted to find that you are working in Austin also. You're the only one of the Harrises who is still single?"

He threw back his head and laughed. "And how do you know I'm single?"

"I heard you tell the conductor. I live alone, too. And I find it frightfully lonely sometimes, don't you?"

"Yes."

"I work at the telephone company, a very interesting position."

48

"How long have you been with the company?"

"I mar—er, moved away for the job about three years ago. Just before Sally married."

"It's a good job for a lady—if a lady must work."

"I have to help Granny. At eighty, her health is failing. She doesn't know I'm coming today, and she'll be surprised to see me. I came on the spur of the moment; I just decided to make a trip yesterday. Will there be a conveyance to take me on out to Granny's from the depot?"

"You can ride with my family. Hopefully, they'll be at the station to meet me. That is, if they got the card I posted. Otherwise, I'm not sure how I'm to get there myself. We might both be walking the dozen miles."

"That might be fun."

"Or exhausting."

"I've walked it to the drugstore many a time."

"I've walked it, too, but not after a hundred-mile train trip and no food. I didn't have time to eat this morning."

"You've had no *food*?" She rummaged in her handbag. "Here. I brought some cookies, never dreaming I'd get to share them with a nice gentleman. I ate a good meal before I left."

"You've just saved my life!" Alan took the refreshments she offered.

"I'm anxious to get reacquainted with the entire Harris family. I consider our meeting more than happenstance. We can have some great times together while we are home. I'll ask Granny to have you over for a meal."

Things were going better than Molly had planned.

CHAPTER SIX

Meeting the Train

Martha pulled off her bleach-faded apron and patted at the waves of gray hair that culminated in a tight knot at the back of her head. "Ever'one should be here by a-Sunday," she said. "We can all church t'gether. Now who's to stay where? Dessie, you an' yorn are a'ready here—"

When Henry was alive, the Harris reunion was always held on Thanksgiving. The crops laid by, he said he would have more leisure time to enjoy his family. But now that he was gone, the children voted to have it in the spring. The weather was more agreeable, they said, and they wanted to be with their mother around the grave on the anniversary of their father's burial.

The last three gatherings had been somewhat depressing to Sally without her father, but this year she felt differently. Arthur had been missing last year, Dessie the year before. Now, they'd all be together.

"Matthew and Pauline will want to go to the Stevenses' and be with her folks," Sarah said. "And William and Nellie will want to stay with the Gibsons. Wherever we stay, we'll be but a hand's turn away.''

"I'll keep Arthur and Lucy," Sally offered. "They're nearer mine and Jay's ages. And I can keep Chester, too. Likely as not, his wife won't come. She never does.''

"Then I'll keep Joseph's bunch," said Sarah.

"Alan," spoke up Martha, "will stay right here with me, of course. We'll have our big dinners here.'' She looked at Sally. "You *did* ask Elise Young t' go along with usns t' meet Alan's train t-day, didn't you, Sally-girl?''

"I did, Mama. In fact, I *insisted* that she come along, but she begged to be excused. She said she had work to do at the school.''

"She gets paid fer school hours an' no extry," fumed Martha. "I don't see why she feels duty bound to spend her free time in th' classroom. Nobody asks it of her ner expects it.'' She paused. "An' this bein' a Friday at that.''

"This is her first assignment, and she wants to do good. She's a dedicated teacher.''

"She's takin' her job too serious. She needs some flockin' with her own kind. Some parties. Some courtin'.''

"I couldn't drag her along by her hair, Mama.''

"Well, we've a-plenty a-time fer match makin', I s'pose. We can't rush Providence.''

"Providence isn't what needs rushing.'' Sally brushed back a stray curl. "It's Alan that needs the hurry-up. He's almost thirty years old.''

Dessie looked up from the skirt she hemmed, pulling a knot in the thread. "Yes, and did you know that there's a thirty-percent chance that a thirty-year-old will *never* get married? That's statistics.''

"You're saying that a third of all thirty-year-olds will be hopeless bachelors?''

52

"That's exactly my point."

"Whose statistics is that?"

"Aw, it's something Dessie made up." Sarah moistened her fingers to thread another needle for her sister.

"Check it out," suggested Dessie.

"So I suppose forty percent reach bachelorhood by forty and fifty percent by age fifty—and one hundred percent by one hundred?"

"No," Dessie said. "The rate goes up after thirty. It's fifty percent by age forty and *ninety* percent by age fifty."

"An' two hunnerd percent by age one hunnerd," Martha calculated.

"Something like that, I'm sure, Mama."

The air was thick with unspoken thoughts.

"Do you think Elise smelled a mouse when you asked her to accompany us?" This came from Sarah.

"No. I'm always asking her to go places with me," Sally said. "Sometimes she does, and sometimes she doesn't. Elise has a mind of her own. A *duty-bound* mind. I think if she'd have thought of romance, she would have dropped everything and come along to the station. Romance just doesn't cross her mind. She's too . . . too wrapped up in the children she teaches. If there's such a thing as being too unselfish, Elise is! She never thinks of Elise Young."

"Then we'll have to think of her for her."

"Where do we start thinking?"

"Sarah can throw a party," Martha planned out loud. "I'd give one here, but that'd be *too* see-throughish. Since Sarah's children are Elise's students, she would feel obligated t' attend fer their sakes."

"I like that idea, Mama," Sarah said. "We'll make

53

ice cream and play games. There's nothing more romantic on a spring evening. We'll keep the party going until late. Then Alan can walk Elise home. He's always been a gentlemanly sort."

The sound of Hank's heavy boots cut in on the scheming women. "It's time to head for town, girls. We wouldn't want to stand Alan up at the depot."

"Yes, because if we're a minute late, he'll start walkin'," Martha said.

"And cut across the Dobb's place not knowing the bull is there . . ."

"You can talk on the way, ladies," urged Hank, herding them toward the waiting wagon. "We're taking William's big Conestoga because I don't know how much luggage Alan will have. Last time he brought along a whole trunk of gifts, and I had to make two trips in the buggy."

Sarah, Dessie, Sally, and Matilda climbed into the back of the wagon while Hank gently lifted Martha—as if she were made of fine china—into the seat beside himself. He patted her hand. "The queen of the Harrises," he teased, and she knew he meant it as a compliment.

Alan's train was late.

As the minutes caked into an hour, Martha complained to Sally, "Ifn we'd knowed it was gonna be this tardy, we coulda waited till Elise got through her after-school work an' brung her along with us."

"But we didn't know, Mama."

Matilda, standing in the door of the station, heard the first whistle of the train, muted by distance. "It's coming, Gra'ma!" she cried, trying without success to keep her feet still. "Alan's train is coming!" The child's ex-

uberance suggested that Alan had bought the whole locomotive and would be the sole passenger.

Her face fell when the conductor appeared on the platform with an elderly lady who fussed with her silk handbag and umbrella as the patient man led her down the
ramp.

"It isn't Alan's train!" Matilda said, her eyes filling
with tears. "It's the lady's."

"Lawsy, pet," chided Martha, "there's room on the
train for more than one person!"

Alan was the last off, closely flanked by a smiling
Molly. He took his suitcase—and hers—from the
attendant.

"Well, look who's on the same train with Alan!" Sally whispered to Sarah. "I haven't seen Molly since she
married that frightful Eli Adams—the man from the telephone company—months ago. She's made herself scarce
around here for the last three years. Wonder what brings
her back now?"

"I'm surprised her marriage has lasted all this time,"
returned Sarah. "I guess she came back to check on her
grandmother's will. Granny Myrt has been failing this last
year. Some say she has the farm and everything she pos-
sesses willed to Molly. Maybe Myrt sent for her."

"Miss Rushing needs a ride to Brazos Point," they
heard Alan tell Hank. "I told her I was sure there would
be a place for her and we would be glad to accommodate
her."

Molly's red lips parted. "Alan is just *so nice*," she
babbled. "I'd forgotten just how nice, really. I find it so
fortunate that we have become reacquainted today and
just the finest of luck that we have come home *together*
. . . ."

Bells of warning rang in Martha's head. *Miss Rushing?* Hadn't she told Alan that she was a married woman and her name was *Adams?* Or—a shiver hit Martha, and she shook although the temperature was quite high today—was Molly no longer married? And had she set in to woo and win Alan Harris?

Molly stayed very near Alan, holding out her hand to be assisted into the back of William's wagon.

Hank stepped to Martha's side to help her into the front seat again. "No!" Martha stood rooted, immovable. "Let Alan ride up here with you, Hank. He's just come home an' you two have a lot o' catchin' up to do. He'll want t' know ifn th' fish is bitin'."

"By no means, First Lady!" Hank laughed. "You get the comfortable place, always. Alan is young, and the bumps in back won't bother him a bit."

"I'd rather have ever' bone in my body disjointed than have my son ride b'side that flapper," she whispered and made a wry face. "Put him up here with you, I say."

"Say, Alan," Hank whistled to the young man already crawling over the wagon's tailgate, extending his hand to Molly, "ride up with me, will you? We have some catching up to do."

"But what . . . what about Mama?"

"Your mother wants to ride back with the girls. It's her special request. We'll humor her this time."

Was it relief that Martha saw on Alan's face? Or was it disappointment?

Molly, apparently miffed at the loss of male attention, said little on the ride to Brazos Point. She did whisper to Sally, though, that Eli Adams had left her months earlier and she hoped never to see him again. She and Sally had shared their darkest of secrets in girlhood days.

She planned, she said, to tell her grandmother that she had buried her husband. It wasn't exactly a lie. Her love for him had died, and she was burying the past. "And you're to keep my secret." She demonstrated the demand with a hand across her mouth, zipper fashion.

Martha heard none of the low conversation, but her spirit was troubled. When Matilda called her attention to the bluebonnets, her eyes only paused for tiny moments of concentration then seemed not to see the flowers at all. "You're not listening to me, Gra'ma," Matilda accused.

"No, lamb. Gra'ma has lots o' unnervy things t' think on right now."

Whatever her status, Molly's "visit" couldn't have come at a worse time.

CHAPTER SEVEN

The Party

"Alan can take me on to Granny Myrt's," Molly said when they reached the Harris farm just before sundown. "I could walk were it not for my heavy suitcase. Alan said he wouldn't mind at all—" It wasn't exactly what Alan had said.

"It will be no problem for me to take you on," Hank said quickly when he saw Martha's mouth set tightly like a steel trap. "It'll save switching around. Alan will want to unpack his things and get settled before bedtime." He hurried the last Harris passenger out, kept Matilda with him, and set the horses to a trot toward Myrt's place.

"I think I'd like to take a little walk around to refresh my memories of the old home place before dark." Alan set his luggage on the porch and stretched his arms. "After the hectic city life, it'll make me feel like a neglected plant being watered."

"Help yerself, Alan. Yore home." *Of all my sons, he's th' easiest on th' eyes,* Martha thought. *An' he was sech a runt when he was born, I thought he wouldn't draw breath more'n a week!* She watched him run his hand through his thick, wavy hair. *He stands tall an' looks jest right in his clothes. Why any suit would be plumb proud to sit acrost them shoulders. . . .* Her eyes followed as he ambled off toward the barn, whistling a hymn. *He seems happy. An', dear God, let his happiness have nothin' t' do with this impertinent Molly. . . .*

"I'll bound ye he needs jest a few quiet moments," Martha said to no one in particular. "He'll be back in a wee bit t' tell all sorts of excitin' stories 'bout life in th' city."

But it was well after dark when Alan came humming back—and from a different direction. He came down the road. He'd been down to the bridge, Martha told herself and hoped it was true.

Alan's absence had given the plotting women a chance to schedule their party for the next evening. "We need to make every minute count," Dessie concluded. "It seems Elise may have a little competition."

"I'll get word to Elise about the party," Sarah said. "I'll send one of the children with a hand-printed invitation."

"Joseph and Amy should be in from the Territory by morning. The more the merrier."

"It's funny that we still call it th' Territory, ain't it?" reminded Martha. "When it's been made into a state an' named New Mexico now. I guess it'll always be th' Territory to usns an' we'll always call Joseph an' Amy our Territory tribe!"

On Saturday morning, Alan said he planned to do some fishing while he was home if he could work it in. He found some hooks in the barn and made a trot line.

"The old yellow cats still biting in the same hole?" he asked Hank.

"Pulled a big one out just last week. Crappie are running, too."

"You have permission to go fishing, Alan, but you must be home in time for a party we've planned at Sarah's at six o'clock." Sally made the proclamation. "We're having ice cream and games."

"Never fear. I'll be back for Mama's country supper," he said. "*That* I'd be less inclined to miss than a party."

By midafternoon, he was home, all smiles and good cheer. He got dressed and left for Sarah's house as soon as supper was over, arriving there almost an hour early.

Sarah met him at the door. "Michael went and sprained his ankle today, Alan. A pretty nasty turn. It's swollen badly. I'll have Chester take a look at it when he gets here. I hope nothing is broken. But Michael wants you to come up to his room and visit for a few minutes before the party gets started. I didn't think you'd mind to say him a quick hello."

Alan took the stairs to the attic room two at a time.

Fifteen-year-old Michael looked up from his home-chiseled chess game. "Hi, Uncle Alan!"

"Who's winning—you or you?"

Michael grinned. "I was just practicing up until you got here to give me a challenge. Here, you take the black. Or had you rather have the white?"

"Either." Alan pulled up a cane-bottomed chair and was soon lost in the game. By the time the first match ended, the crowd was gathering below.

"I can't take this foot downstairs, Uncle," Michael apologized. "I wish you could just stay up here and keep me company. It's lonesome here. There's plenty of people for the games downstairs and just me by myself in this room. That doesn't seem fair, does it?"

"No," Alan hesitated. "But I wouldn't want to seem antisocial."

"Oh, pooh. There'll be plenty more family doings. You just but got here yesterday."

"Yes, and I'm jostled by so many people in the city, I rather like the quiet in your corner of the world."

"Then just stay and play with me."

"You twisted my arm."

"We can have our own party."

A door opened below, bringing the sound of a voice that echoed an octave higher than the others: "Granny Myrt told me you were having a party," it chirped, "and she said I should join. I think she wanted me out of the house so she could go to bed early. I'm a night person. I knew you wouldn't mind me joining the fun. . . ." The voice moved away and mingled with the other voices. "Where's Alan?"

Molly Rushing.

"Who's that?" Michael's words came out in a half-whisper.

"That's Sister Myrt's granddaughter."

"The one who married the telephone man?"

"No. This one isn't married."

"Oh. I thought Granny Myrt only had one grand-daughter—a Mrs. Adams."

"She must have more than one. Molly is quite young. Early twentyish, probably. And a pretty girl, too—especially her eyes."

"Do you like her?"

Alan, always careful to set a Christian example for all his nephews, pondered the question before he answered. "She's a little . . . uh, modern. But one doesn't dislike people just because they have different values. I don't know her well yet, but I think she could be quite a lovely person. Does that answer your question?"

"Not exactly, but let's play another game of chess and forget about girls."

Sally came up the stairs first. "There you are, Alan!" She sighed with the relief of one who had found a long-lost object. "Sarah thought you might still be up here with Michael. Miss Young and the Stevenses are here, and we're waiting for you to join the party."

"If you'll have me excused please, Sally. Michael isn't up to the festivities tonight, so I promised to keep him company. You might be so kind as to send Becky and Matilda up with bowls of ice cream for the two of us while we play at our game here. If it isn't too much bother . . ."

"But—"

"And tell Grandma Harris that Alan is going to stay the night with me, too, Aunt Sally, so she won't worry when he doesn't show up at home tonight."

Sally left frowning.

Sarah came up next. "Michael, you can get along without Alan," she scolded. "It isn't right for you to keep him from socializing just because you're laid up."

"Oh, this is my idea of a good time, Sarah!" objected Alan with unguarded honesty. "It's as much my fault as it is his. It's been ages since I've unwound with a good game of chess. That comes of living by myself too long. And chess is one of my favorite games." His eyes twinkled. "And besides being one of my favorite people, Michael is a pro at this game! Nothing boring here."

Sarah left unhappy, too.

"They want you downstairs something fierce, don't they?" Michael noticed.

"Seems that way." Alan clucked his tongue. "Women are funny creatures, Michael. They have no idea how transparent they are. Ten to one they are trying to match me up with somebody. Ma and my sisters have been trying to marry me off for years."

"Yipes! I hope they never try that on me. Do you ever plan to get a wife?"

"I'm sure I will, when the time is right. But to find a lifetime mate begs a lot of praying and being sure. One can't afford to make the wrong choice—"

"Like Uncle Chester?"

"That really wasn't who I had in mind. I always thought my favorite Bible character struck a bad match."

"Who's that?"

"David. He was a country boy at heart, and he married a city girl. David and the king's daughter didn't have much in common—she a real princess and he a poor shepherd boy. I've wondered what attracted Michal to David in the first place. I suppose it was the generic female weaknesses. David was good to look upon and fearless. When he returned from his giant-slaying tournament, gals flocked about him with a sort of hero worship: singing, dancing, calling his name."

"Probably embarrassed him, didn't it?"

"I imagine it did. But Michal liked cheering crowds, stardom, the limelight. I doubt if she gave David a second look when he sat shepherd-cloaked and barefoot on a Judean hill, playing his harp for Jehovah.

"The brave hero days and the king-crowning days pleased her vanity. But she didn't appreciate David's religion. What David loved the most, she hated the worst.

"A woman who is in love with her husband wants to share in his dreams, his ambitions, his victories. David had a dream as every man does. Who was it that said, 'Respect a man for his dreams as much as for his performance'? David's dream was to bring the ark of God back to its rightful place in Jerusalem.

"David behaved as a foolish sentimentalist to Michal. And when he expressed in a spontaneous dance his unrestrained joy about getting back the ark, she actually despised him in her heart. He had come home with the grand intention of blessing everyone, but she slapped him with scorn!

"It was such an unfortunate marriage. So sad. David sang his last recorded song alone."

Michael sat in deep thought, affected by what Alan had said.

"I see what you mean, Uncle Alan. And you think this party tonight is a scheme?"

"It may be or it may not be. Sally surely fried up my shirt nicely."

"No wonder she's miffed. Here you sit in my room with nobody to see your starchy shirt. All her work for nothing!"

"Your room is a haven for me tonight, Michael. And I may need your help in the future."

"I'm sitting on ready."

Molly's voice left early when it became apparent that Alan had absented himself from the social gathering and would not be joining them.

Eventually the other guests began to leave.

"The party's breaking up, Alan."

Dessie came up the stairs last. "Miss Young and the Stevenses and Mama are getting ready to go. Mama says you might want to walk over home tonight and get your trousers for church tomorrow."

"If Mama needs an escort, I'll be glad to see her home. Are Sally and Jay here to walk with her and see that she's safe?"

"Yes, but—"

"Then I'll just stay. I'm an early riser. Tell Mama I'll be over before breakfast in the morning to get ready for church."

CHAPTER EIGHT

Disappointing Sunday

The kitchen was filled with rich, yeasty odors. Martha served so many varieties of jelly and jam that Alan called her "five-course breakfast table" the stomach's library.

After the meal, the family dressed for church. Alan wore gray trousers, a gray vest, and a darker gray coat. Martha's eyes suffered pride as she looked at him. How had he escaped the traps of cunning heart-hunters this long?

Alan would meet Elise Young today, and what better place to meet than at God's house? Martha would invite the teacher to sit with them then have her over for Sunday dinner to meet all the family. In the afternoon, they'd sit out on the sun-warmed porch and—

"Are you ready, Mama?" Alan took her arm and guided her across the yard. *As ifn I was breakable or helpless,* she thought, relishing every minute of it. They met Sarah's family at the road and all went "towardsing" the church together as Matilda would say. Wild flowers wove themselves into a multicolored pattern along the way. If only Henry could be here this morning to enjoy his children! Martha took time for the one brief regret. Sundays were his favorite days. But perhaps he was looking on from his perch in the sky.

While the parishioners mingled in greeting, Martha found Elise and suggested that she share the Harris family's section of pews since she had no family of her own.

"How kind of you, Mrs. Harris!" She gave a lovely, genteel smile. "But Pastor Stevens has asked that I have a special session just for the children this morning since the sanctuary is so crowded. I'm happy to oblige our pastor. I'll take the young ones across the road to the schoolhouse and tell them one of my favorite Bible stories. I'll be glad to sit with you at another time."

"Has he—Pastor Stevens—asked—that is, will you need someone t'—er—t' help you?"

"I think I can manage the children. I'm accustomed to them every day of the week. But thank you for your offer." Her small laugh sounded musical.

"I'll—I'll see if I can get someone t' help you get them settled in at least—"

"Oh, I'll be fine."

"Would you like t' take dinner at my house with our family t'day, Miss Young?"

The girl's crockery blue eyes lighted, making her sweet, ungarnished face even brighter. "Why, I'd *love* it, Mrs. Harris! It would be my pleasure to be sure—if you're sure you haven't your hands quite full already."

"I never seen a Harris table what didn't have room fer one more."

Martha found Alan smothered by Molly and Grandmother Myrt. "Alan, could you help with the children this morning?"

"It would be my delight, Mama, but Pastor Stevens has asked that I lead the congregation in song to begin the service," he said. "I'm sure Jay or Hank would be more than happy to be of assistance." Alan turned his attention back to what Molly was saying. The look on the girl's rouged face said she had claimed and branded Martha's last single son.

A flustered Martha fought a spasm of resentment followed by a sprout of panic. Her vexation roped in the pastor, Sister Myrt, Molly, and any other unseen force that worked against her. She set her jaw and immediately resolved to do whatever it took to put a stop to a romance between this girl and her son. Alan would *not* marry a pre-owned trollop!

Alan's deeply pitched voice leading out on "He Leadeth Me" failed to assuage Martha's inner turmoil. Her mind was a whirlpool in a turbulent, unruly river of plans and roadblocks. Brother Stevens's sermon was wasted on her unheeding ears. Joseph, sensing her unrest, reached over to pat her hand. Joseph, her oldest—the most like Henry. If only he understood!

But he didn't. Nobody understood. How could they? But wait! God did. Why hadn't she thought to share her fears with her heavenly Father? She closed her eyes, formed an unspoken plea in prayer, and sent it heavenward marked "urgent."

She felt somewhat better. After all, Elise would be going home with them for dinner, she told herself, and Alan would have all afternoon to see her virtues for himself. He would recognize that she was in all points superior to the superficial Molly. Alan was a perceptive young man; he'd always read people well. He would be quick to analyze Elise's worth.

Wind blew in the open windows and ruffled the leaves of the parson's Bible. Martha's gaze drifted toward the schoolhouse.

Church ended without Martha's absorbing a single spiritual nugget. William gave the benediction, and the crowd again mingled in greetings and reminiscenses. Babies were crooned over, children commended on their growth since last year, newcomers presented and introduced.

Only William's wife, Nellie, seemed quiet and withdrawn. Her eyes held a haunted faraway look. A sort of hunger, Martha decided. Her face, usually high-colored and good-humored, was drawn and white. She looked miserable.

She's ill, thought Martha with alarm. *My William's wife is sick. An', oh, if anything should happen t' her, I'd have William t' bury, too!*

The schoolhouse door swung open, and a horde of jubilant children flocked out, followed by their teacher. The sun caught in Elise's golden hair, turning it to finely spun gold. It almost seemed that a halo hung about her head. Martha looked around to see if Alan saw the miracle, but he was cloistered just inside the church doors, nodding to Sister Myrt.

He gave a quick glance toward his mother, as if searching for her, then hurried her direction.

"Sister Myrt has prepared a picnic lunch for Molly, herself, and me," he said. "It would be most impolite of me to refuse her invitation, don't you think?"

"But Alan! I've invited—that is, I had planned for you t' eat with th' family on yore first Sunday home—"

"We'll have plenty of meals together during the week, Mama dear. Chester isn't here yet, so I won't exactly be breaking the circle. I can't be ungracious when the dear old soul has gone to so much trouble and effort just for me."

"Alan, I do need t' talk t' you about—" Before Martha had time to stutter her warning about Molly, the young woman was tugging at Alan's sleeve.

"Granny's ready, Alan." And he was gone. *With her.*

Elise donned an apron and helped Martha put dinner on the round oak table worn with much polishing. Everything about the teacher was quick and light and alive. She didn't fill the air with tiresome chatter like most of her generation did, but she was pleasant and easy to be around. It was evident that the whole family enjoyed her company.

Martha made great effort to rein in her thoughts, wishing for Alan. Perhaps if she kept Elise the evening, he would dismiss himself from Myrt's devious picnic early and bring himself on home.

"I had planned for *all* my fam'ly who've come in t' eat t'gether t'day," Martha said. "I wanted you t' meet them. But my son Alan was invited somewhere else. It's not like he's a child an' I can still tell him what to do . . ." Her laugh was nervous. "Though I'd sometimes like to! A man nigh thirty might resent bein' mama-bossed."

"And you have another son yet to arrive for the reunion, Mrs. Harris?"

"Yes, an' that's my Chester. He's Alan's twin. I don't know ifn his wife will come er not. Likely not. She ain't

71

very comfortable with our country ways." Martha made quick amends lest Elise think her critical of her son's wife. "She's a nice young lady, though. She jest ain't accustomed to usns. She's always had a cityfied life an' she—she don't understand usns."

"You have a lovely family," Elise said, her compliment taking in everyone. "It must be nice to have so many. I was a rather lonely child. Mother went on to heaven, along with a baby brother, before I had a chance to know either of them. I've always been intrigued by large families."

"Yore papa never took on another wife?"

"No, ma'am. I suppose the rearing of me took up his time and energy. He's gone, too, now."

"He did a powerful good job on you."

"Thank you, Mrs. Harris. I hope I've made a daughter he wouldn't be ashamed to introduce to the angels."

Martha stretched the serving, eating, and cleanup as long as she could. Surely Alan would be in soon. Each metered twang of the grandfather clock, gonging out another hour, plunged her heart lower and lower. Finally, Elise excused herself and went home, thanking Martha graciously for including her in the family gathering.

Henry always accused Martha of "inventing" worries. But some worries manufactured themselves, she contended. Besides the fret over Alan, Martha now had Nellie to consider. William's wife had hardly touched her plate today. Her eyes seemed only a step from the splash of tears.

She found William in the cow lot. "Is Nellie ailin', William?" she asked.

"It's a heart sickness, Mama." William cleaned the

sole of his boot on the hay. "In counting her blessings, she comes up one short. She wants a child so badly she aches. She thought she was in a family way, but yesterday she knew she wasn't. It most nigh broke her heart. She took the disappointment sorely. I wish I could say something to help her or to comfort her. Crowds make it worse—seeing families worship together and play together. Seeing Lucy's baby . . . And with Lucy only married two years to Nellie's dozen."

Martha laid her blue-veined hand on William's brawny arm. "Listen to me, son. God has plenty o' souls in His mind that needs sortin' an' taggin'. He's got one—an' mayhap more—tagged as William an' Nellie's—same as He has a wife tagged as Alan's."

And, as far as Martha was concerned, that summed up the matter. But as she walked back toward the house, a nagging fear dropped its plow into her heart. What if Alan didn't read the tag right?

She was sure the tag wouldn't say *Molly*.

CHAPTER NINE

Chester's Advice

Chester *looked* the same, Alan thought, but he *acted* differently. Pensive. More reserved. Less relaxed.

He seemed glad to be in the country but unable to wind down to its slower pace. He and Alan had always been close, and Alan sensed a spiritual coldness, as if Chester's soul had begun to rust out and he was slowly dying with some dread ulcer. Whatever the wall Chester had built, Alan planned to batter it down.

He caught a time to do this late one evening when everyone else had put up for the night. He found Chester on the front veranda alone: a large and frameless bulk staring into the dark, implacable sky. Evening creatures, making sounds like a tightly strung fiddle, sang and sobbed and chirped in the black atmosphere.

"Chester."

His brother turned with a slow, ponderous motion. Finally he spoke. "I couldn't sleep, brother. Sit down and let's visit awhile. I get hungry to talk to you. How's the work going in Austin?"

"Little has changed."

"Sometimes slow changes are better than abrupt ones."

"When we chop down one inconsistency, two more crop up to take its place." Alan chuckled. "People are migrating to Texas en masse since the oil boom. More people mean more work for the lawmakers."

"Stay with it, Alan. We need good men like you."

"But I want to hear about your work, Chester."

"You knew I finished medical school?"

"Mama wrote me. Congratulations."

"I'm working with my brother-in-law right now, but Candice is urging me to get out and practice on my own."

"You surprised us all when you decided to become a doctor. Not that we didn't think you'd make the world's best—and we're all proud of you—but jumping from road construction to the medical profession was a big change, wasn't it?"

"Yes, and I'm sure I'd never have made the jump on my own. I have Candice to thank for the encouragement—or nagging—whichever you want to call it. She declared me badly miscast as a bricklayer."

"Being a doctor is not something you chose—that you enjoy?"

"Helping the hurting . . . that I like. I would like going from house to house, being an old-fashioned doctor, taking blackberry jelly for remuneration—"

"Then by all means, find yourself a place like our home county here and dig in your heels! It's a big world, and your profession isn't a congested one. I'm told the demand exceeds the supply by several hundred, and some rural areas are desperate for a doctor."

"Unfortunately, that's not the kind of doctor Candice has in mind for me to be. There's no money in it."

"*Money?* Doctors are public servants. Like preachers. They take whatever they can get. What did our old doc used to say? 'Twenty dollars a month in cash and two hundred in gratitude.'"

"Candice has to have money, Alan. Cold cash. She insists that I become a specialist."

"A what?"

"That's a doctor trained in one particular field of medicine. The trend for the future. For instance, I might study to be a bone doctor. I would know all about bones: how to set them, treat them, reset them, medicate them. Another doctor might learn all about the respiratory system. The lungs, breathing, congestive complaints: asthma, pneumonia, bronchitis, pulmonary problems. Patients would get special, expert care from someone who had the expertise for that particular case—"

"It's unthinkable, Chester! Absurd! Say I broke my leg and called for a doctor and the doctor in my area happened to be a head doctor or a stomach doctor or a skin doctor. What good would he do me if he knew nothing about my *leg?* That system would mean a dozen doctors to the one we have now—and we're already short-handed and—"

When Alan paused to reload his verbal gun, Chester stopped him. "Dr. Sharp, my brother-in-law, says that there's no future in house calls, anyway. Someday, that will be a thing of the past. Old hat."

"Don't let him brainwash you, Chester. People will always need a doctor to come to them when they get sick or injured. Especially children. That's just hardpan common sense."

"There will be specified places for them to go to be treated, Alan. Hospitals. Clinics. Doctors' offices. Sanitariums."

"But what if—what if a man is not able to make the trip? Suppose it's miles away to such an institution? Every small town will not be able to afford such an extravagance."

"I don't know. I suppose that would be his problem."

"Callous thinking! Barbaric. I hope to see a law against it."

"It's coming sooner or later, Alan. You can't buck it."

"I tell you, it won't work. And I'll buck it as long as I have breath in my lungs."

"They told the Wright brothers their flying machine wouldn't work, either."

"We're not talking about *machinery*, Chester. We're talking about human lives—real people."

"There will still be some general practitioners, probably forever. But they will be for ordinary ills and ails. Surgeries done in homes are often performed under unsanitary conditions. Doctors sometimes don't have the proper equipment on hand and cannot carry it around with them. According to my brother-in-law, a lot more lives will be saved with the hospital system. Especially cases of a more serious nature."

"And a lot lost trying to get there. Plus the expense. Will this be only for those who can *afford* to live? What will the poor do?"

"All these factors will be worked out. Probably through some form of insurance or hospitalization plan paid in small amounts before an emergency arises."

"At best, it will be a headache!"

"Yes, and that's why I said I would like to be a circuit-riding country doctor. These things weigh heavily on my mind."

"Do what your heart dictates, Chester."

Chester gave a satirical smile. "With a wife like Candice, you do what Candice dictates. She would never agree to live in the country. She's city to the core. She thrives on parties, clubs, society friends. I can't even get her to come to a family reunion with me in the country once a year. Forty miles from the throng is a universe away."

"As I recall, she came the first year you were married."

"And if you'll recall, she hasn't been back since. She said she would never accompany me here again. My family is 'too primitive' for her tastes. If pride is a germ, she is sick. She can't abide Mama's poor English, our home-spun manners—" To admit these facts scalded Chester's soul with bitter acid. Alan hoped that the spilling out of the hurts might help.

"Didn't she know your background when she married you? You were still working for the street-paving crew with no degrees following your name when she agreed to be your wife."

"She thought she could change me. She could mold me to her liking. And she has." His voice softened. "She has made of me a better person, and I have to thank her for that. I would never have gotten past the first semester without her pushing and pulling. But I feel fragmented and torn. I hate the formality her family imposes upon me and its hypocrisy. How did Papa put it? You can take the boy out of the country, but you can't take the country out of the boy. Candice's ambition is that not a trace of country be left in my bones."

"It's not fair, Chester."

"But I have one antidote. I'm happy when I'm lost in my work. When I see my patients, especially little children, healthy and healed again, I feel a great sense of satisfaction and accomplishment. Then I'm leading a worthwhile life. I'm a good doctor, Alan, like you are good in legislation."

"I'm . . . I'm sorry about Candice."

"None of us can have all the good shakes in life. I find that sometimes the bitter makes the sweet even sweeter. I should have asked God about my marriage. But who knows? He might have sided with Candice. It probably took a woman like her to head me in the right direction, however expensive the journey."

"Has Candice decided what you should specialize in?"

"She wants me to be a heart surgeon. But—pardon the pun—my heart isn't in it. I want to be a pediatrician."

"That's a—"

"Children's doctor. In the new scope of medicine, there'll be doctors for various segments of society. Women's doctors. Children's doctors . . . We have three graves in the cemetery now, and two of them are children's: our own little brother and Sarah's firstborn. Too many children die needlessly, before they have a chance at life."

"What about your spiritual life, Chester? Are you attending church?"

"I'm . . . I'm afraid my soul isn't well, Alan. And you needn't tell me that a soul is more important than a body, because I already know that. Candice wasn't reared to love God as we were. I get nothing out of the dead, formal church she holds membership with. If I wanted to know the humanitarian woes of the world, I'd read the newspaper! When I go to church, I want to hear a message from the Bible, not a rehearsed sermon. Sermons and messages are different. I like to hear from God."

"Go to your own church, Chester. You can find one—"

"I see that you don't understand, brother."

"Nothing should come between you and God."

"Candice would make life so miserable for me—" Chester chopped off his sentence and said no more.

They sat in silence, each thinking his own thoughts. Then Alan steered the conversation away from the fester, knowing that all he could do was pray for this brother with whom he had shared clothes, resin gum, and a wooden top. His grief he could not truly share.

"Do you know a Miss Molly Rushing, Chester?"

"Granny Myrt's granddaughter?"

"Yes."

"Don't remember much about her. She lived with her mother off somewhere part of the time, didn't she?"

"She's a few years younger than we are, so I don't recall much of her family history. She said she finished school with Sally."

"Didn't she marry a telephone man?"

"No. She isn't married. But she does work for the telephone company. In Austin."

"Let me think. It's coming back to me now. I do believe she *did* get married. Seems it was the same year Sally and Jay wed. And you say she's single again?"

"Well, she seems to be. She didn't mention a husband or ever having had one."

"I'd wager a guess that if she did marry, her husband

got killed. He had a high risk job climbing poles. Well, poor little Molly. And I guess she took back her maiden name. I remember when she made me sodas at the drugstore for free. She was always a generous little thing. And friendly. Why do you ask?"

"She came in on the same coach as I did. To visit her grandmother. Of course, I had no way of knowing about her husband's being dead. It must be something she doesn't want to discuss. That's the way some people handle their grief—mutely. She was open enough about everything else."

"Speaking of women, Alan, I don't know if you ever plan to marry. But let me give you some brotherly advice. Choose a woman, whatever her past, who will attend your family reunions with you." Loneliness and longing honed the words.

Alan laughed to ease the tension. "Okay. That's the first promise I'll extract from her, Chester. 'Do you promise, before God and these witnesses, to attend the annual Harris reunion? . . .'"

CHAPTER TEN

Disconcerting News

During the second week of Alan's home visit, Molly staged a "sing" at her grandmother's place and invited all the young folks. All, that is, except Elise Young.

Thinking that Elise with her lovely soprano voice would surely be there, Martha urged Alan to go. "We've several more days t'gether," she said, "and you need t' flock with feathers of yore own brilliance. Go along an' sing a note er two fer me. When I was young, singin's was my cup o' tea."

She smelled his spicy shaving lotion as he went out the front door and smiled to herself. Tonight . . .

But a series of disconcerting happenings caused Martha's good humor to hemorrhage badly that evening.

First, Elise knocked at the door with a card in her hand.

"Mrs. Harris," she said, "the mailman put this card in the wrong box. It is for your son and must have gotten tangled among my school catalogues." She handed it to Martha. "One never knows when a message may be important."

"My, my!" exclaimed Martha, flustered. "Mr. Richmond is in such a hurry t' get home now'days that he scarcely looks at th' backin' on our letters. Yesterday, some of Sarah's mail got in with mine. But it's excusable since th' man's wife has been so ill. He knows he can trust usnst' straighten it out fer him."

"How is his wife, Mrs. Harris?"

"Some say she has black leg. But I hear she's some better, . . ." Martha's recalcitrant mind pulled up some discrepancy as she looked at Elise. "But why . . . why aren't you at th' sing?"

Elise's delicate cheeks colored. "Miss Rushing doesn't know me, Mrs. Harris."

"You mean you didn't even get an invite?"

"I shouldn't expect to. I'm new here and haven't become well acquainted with the granddaughter of Granny Myrt—"

"What better way t' get acquainted? I can't b'lieve Molly would have overlooked you. And with your beautiful voice. I hope it wasn't deliberate."

"Oh, I'm sure it wasn't. But it makes no matter, Mrs. Harris. Truly it doesn't. I have a new book that I needed to look over anyhow—"

"It *does* matter." Martha wrinkled the postcard with the force of her words. "Please sit down, Miss Young. I need to talk t' someone b'fore I work myself up into a lather an' have another apoplexy attack."

"Please don't be upset, Mrs. Harris. So small a thing as a singing doesn't merit the fret."

"That's jest th' tail tip o' th' skunk!" Martha said and pointed Elise to the porch swing. "Molly Rushin' is after my son. A blind man could see that. An' she's . . . she's not worthy of him!"

"Being a son of Martha Harris, I'm sure he has a good sense of discernment."

"But he doesn't know how wily Molly can be, Miss Elise! Men are easy fooled. It happened t' my Chester." The card was nearly crumpled now. "Molly determined herself t' marry one o' mine when she was yet in pinafores. It was William, then it was Arthur. Now it's Alan. She's been married, an' th' good Lord only knows where she's stashed her husband. Her name ain't Molly Rushin'. It's Molly *Adams*. She married jest b'fore my Sally did. An' it's no hearsay; I was at her weddin', a-sittin' on th' third bench from th' front. An' now she comes back to try to hornswoggle my son into a romance. She follered him here. Oh, this old maw ain't blind. Ner deef. Ner dumb."

"Have you talked to your son about it?"

"Ever'time I try, he jest waves me away an' starts talkin' about somethin' else. I'm afeared he won't realize what she's about until it's too late."

"I offer you my prayers, Mrs. Harris. Please try not to worry."

"But I *do* worry, Miss Elise. Ifn my son marries a flapper like that'n, I'll sink into my grave in six feet o' pure mud an' never be able to get out."

"We'll say a prayer that your son will always take the high road in life. That's the very prayer my father prayed for me."

When Elise took her leave, Martha still held the much abused card in her fist. With an embarassed sigh at the condition of Alan's mail, she tried to smooth it out and in the smoothing turned it over to the message side. Her entire stock of integrity labored to keep her eyes from the private note, but a few of the words at the end leaped off the stiff cardboard to her. "—miss you and have some plans for us when you get back to Austin." It was signed "Affectionately, Helen Jorgensen."

Here was yet another shock. One of those city buzzards had her talons sharpened for Alan Harris. The sort of woman that ran around idle all day. To movie houses. To dance halls. To businesses managed by men. With necklines too low and rolled stockings. Some of them were even taking up cigarette smoking and wine bibbing. Brazen, shameless girls they were! What could be worse?

Martha shuddered. If only she could close Alan in a room and with her own body bar the door against society's vultures. She would permit no painted faces, no flirting eyelids, no cropped hair. She would admit no female company at all for her son, she decided. Except Elise.

Then came Matilda with her story.

"Gra'ma!" she called. "I do think your bestest wish is coming true!"

Martha slid the postcard into her apron pocket out of sight. "What wish, Pet?"

"About Uncle Alan."

"Gra'ma don't know what yore talkin' about, honey."

"You wished on him a wife, didn't you?"

Martha's heart lurched. "Yes, but a *good one*. No floozies."

"I have a secret, but I've been keeping it locked tight. Nobody knows about it but me myself."

"About Alan?"

"Yep."

"Say, 'yes, ma'am,' Tilly."

"Yes, ma'am."

86

"What's yore secret?"

"If I tell it, it won't be a secret anymore, will it?"

"Yes, it'll be a two-person secret. A gra'ma-grand-daughter secret."

"I was out hunting Scaredy-cat because her kittens were mewing and awfully bad hungry—"

"I don't have to hear all about yore cats this time."

"Well, I was just explaining why I was where I was when I was so you wouldn't scold or wonder."

"Okay, I won't scold or wonder. But what does this have t' do with Alan?"

"I was looking *everywhere* for Scaredy-cat, and I started down the trail by the river. I was looking under the bushes and behind the trees and in the tall grass. But I stopped when I saw Uncle Alan and a girl in a checked dress sitting with their heads close together and talking quiet-like right on the riverbank."

"When was this, Tilly?"

"Yesterday. But you had so many people around you yesterday I couldn't tell it."

"Who was th' girl? Was she known t' you?"

"I couldn't tell who she was. I wasn't close enough. She was backed to me, and I couldn't see her face—"

"What color was her hair?"

"I couldn't see that either. She had on a bonnet."

"Did Alan know that you saw him—them?"

"No. The noise of the water hid me. And when I saw he was there I left in a hurry because I knew you wanted him to get a girl and I didn't want to a-fright him off from his job."

"Oh, dear."

"But Gra'ma, why are you frowning? I thought my

87

secret would make you *happy*."

"Sometimes a body gets th' wrong sow by th' ear."

"What does that mean?"

"I hope she was a *good* girl."

" 'Course she was, Gra'ma, or Alan wouldn't have been with her. Would a floozy be wearing a checked dress?"

"I don't know, pet." Martha threw out her hands in a helpless gesture. "I don't know what floozies in disguise wear. All I know is I'm a-feared."

"You could ask him—"

"Oh, no, no. That might make matters worse."

Matilda looked uncomfortable. Then she brightened. "But I did find Scaredy-cat, Gra'ma. Do you know where I found her?"

Martha tried to hear what the child was saying. "N-no."

"Right at home with her kittens!"

"Thank you fer tellin' me." Martha patted Matilda's head and managed an artificial smile. "I'm glad you found yore cat. We'll see what we can do t' make things right."

"Oh, Scaredy-cat's all right now!"

"You run along so's you can git home b'fore dark. I've got some thinkin' to do."

"Don't worry about Scaredy-cat's family! She always comes home to her kittens just before they starve to death."

After Matilda left, Martha creaked away in the porch swing, her thoughts sloshing here and there in a curdled disorder. The scratching stopped dead still with Martha's resolution. She went in to the parlor, yanked off her apron, put on her mail-order shoes, and set off for Myrt's house in a haste.

The singing rollicked from the barn, but Martha went directly to the house, where she found Myrt half asleep in her ancient spider rocker. The old woman roused drowsily.

"Myrt," Martha said, omitting the customary "Sister." "I need to have a little understandin' talk with you 'bout yore granddaughter—"

"Why sure, Martha. Have a seat. There anywhere. The younguns are having a good time tonight. They've about sung me to sleep. Seems like old times. I'm glad to see Molly having such a lovely time here in Brazos Point. Poor darling! Life hasn't been kind to her, but she's a spunky one. She'll snap back to her old self if we can keep these parties going. And I think it so fortunate that she came just when all the other young folks came home, too. Your Alan has been so kind to my little Molly—"

"That's what I came t' talk t' you about, Myrt. My Alan an' yore Molly." Her tone had a serrated edge. "My Henry always allowed that scandal travels faster than a bullet an' spreads wider than buckshot. Molly is a married woman an'—"

"Martha—" the old organist began to weep. "Didn't you know? Haven't you heard? Molly's husband was killed on his job, and it's been so hard for Molly to accept his death. She loved him so! You were at the wedding. You heard Pastor Stevens tie them together until death untied the knot. You saw how crazy Eli was over her—how he carried her so tender-like across the threshold. And now to think that the grim reaper has severed those bonds! Oh, Martha, it's almost too much for an old granny's heart to bear . . ."

"I didn't know, Myrt. It seems to me she hasn't been showin' her grievin'."

89

"She puts on a mighty good front. But the tears flow at night. And I know for a fact that she's been spending a lot of time walking in the woods alone. Pining for her Eli. Why, just yesterday she came in with a big plug tore out of her best checked gingham dress where she'd caught it on a briar. Her pretty red checked dress. And with my eyes so dim, the patching was a chore. I was hard put to fix the hole. But I couldn't ask Molly to do her own work with her grief and anguish."

"She *did?* She tore her checked dress at the river?" Matilida's words about the girl on the river bank with Alan came back to bruise Martha. *A checked dress.* Martha's jaw muscles bunched, let up, bunched again. She opened her mouth to say something, but no more words came.

"Yes, she's bad heart hurt, but I think her meeting up with Alan has been helpful. He said you insisted on his coming over tonight. I'm just ever so grateful to you, Martha. That's what I call a real friend—to send her son out to comfort my sorrowing baby."

Now it was Martha who wiped her eyes but not out of sympathy for Molly. The tears were tears of frustration. Nothing was going as she had planned, not even this visit.

Myrt leaned back and closed her eyes but kept talking, her voice droning on like a recorded cylinder. "God does work in mysterious ways, Martha. It never ceases to amaze me. I'm thinking Molly will need to replace Eli one of these days—and God has put her right in the same town with one of yours. We've always been so close neighbored and all; it might be that something will work out for Alan and Molly.

"Molly has always been a precious girl, straightforward and honest with me in everything. Oh, I know the parson thought she painted up too much and stained her nails too often, but he doesn't understand young folks. They will try out these ridiculous notions, but then they settle down. Molly has never been wild. She made just a perfect little wife for Eli. I blamed a lot of Molly's slow spiritual growth on that daughter of mine who pitched the child back and forth from pillar to post. You'll notice Molly has been very eager to attend church since she's been home. She drinks in everything Pastor Stevens says, and she tells me that when she returns to Austin, she will be going to Alan's church there. . . ."

Martha couldn't bear to hear any more. She wanted to plug her ears and run from the house, from Myrt's bombast. With costly self-control, she excused herself to some unfinished task back home and took her leave. She made a wide circle by the barn and heard Molly's high-pitched voice rise above the rest.

"Chester!" she chirped. "I'm so sorry your wife didn't come with you to your family reunion. How unromantic. Now when I marry a man, I plan to be right with him at every family gathering he has. . . ."

CHAPTER ELEVEN

The Teacher's Revelation

Joseph's wife, Amy, had once taught at the Brazos Point school. She could still remember the heady feeling when she got her first appointment and walked into the classroom for the first time. As the years ticked backward, she saw herself once again prudently choosing the seeds of knowledge to be planted into the fertile minds of her pupils each day. Now some of her former students had children of their own in the same classroom.

She had met Elise Young, the new teacher, at church, and the two established a quick rapport, their common denominator being teaching. Elise was prompt to invite Amy to visit the school she formerly commandeered.

Amy chose a Wednesday for the visit—just before Elise's weeklong spring break that would coincide with Easter and the wrap-up of the Harris reunion. Martha's grandchildren would be distracted.

The school had been remodeled. New desks that joined one another found themselves rooted to the floor with bolts. Each had its own inkwell and an indented place for pencils. A shelflike compartment beneath the top held books and tablets. New blackboards sat against bright walls. A bulletin board provided a display for exemplary work.

Amy arrived early. Elise was already there, setting the room in order. Her hair, held back with two simple combs, framed the elegant features of her patrician face. The blue of her dress, sashed at the waist, complemented her eyes. Her picture could grace the cover of a women's journal.

Amy liked Elise, though she wondered about Elise's background. No one knew much of her past or future. The aura of mystery that surrounded her rather piqued Amy's interest, reminding her of herself. She had come to this small school after the tragic loss of both parents and with nothing but a deep trust in God to direct her uncharted path. She had found true friends. And romance.

"Hello." Amy made her presence known.

Elise's face lighted with a glow from somewhere inside. She seemed always on the verse of smiling, Amy thought. "Come on in, Mrs. Harris. I'm glad you've come to visit today. I've been wanting to become better acquainted with you, but I've been quite busy. We are concluding my first six weeks here and are going into a new one after our Easter break."

"We don't have to do everything all in one six-week period," reminded Amy with a hint of humor.

"Do you get to where you can save some of the excitement for another day? Do you get accustomed to it, Mrs. Harris?"

Amy laughed. "Eventually. You like the work here, don't you?"

"Oh, yes! I was overjoyed when I was assigned to a country school all by myself! But I'm afraid it's only temporary. I was sent out until they could replace Mrs. Weathers with a permanent teacher."

"My assignment here was temporary, too," Amy said. "I got to stay a whole school year, though. Then I married and moved away."

"That was nice, wasn't it?"

"Very. I'm surprised, Miss Young, that with your charm some young man hasn't claimed your hand already!"

An undefinable look crossed Elise's face. Amy thought it a potpourri of hope, faith—and what was the other ingredient? Amy could not decide.

"I am promised," she said timidly, a soft blush creeping across her cheeks as she dropped her eyes. "Before my father died, a man asked for me. And I've considered myself betrothed since that day. Father was such a prayerful, perceptive man—so in tune with God. It was as if he could see into the future and knew just what was best for me. I put utmost trust in him and my heavenly Father."

"But, Miss Young, I'm sure your father wouldn't hold you to such an arrangment!"

"It is my choice to honor his wishes."

"But what if the man who asked for you should change his mind?"

"I don't think it will happen, but if it did, I would pray about another direction for my life or perhaps stay unmarried forever."

"But do you really love—?" Before Amy's question could be completed and answered, the door burst open and a student ran toward Elise swinging a large flour sack.

"Maw sent you some cucumbers, Miss Young. I do hope you enjoy them."

She hugged the child. "Thank you, Tony, I'm sure I will. Give your mother a hug for me."

Amy and Elise had no further leisure for private visiting, and Amy carried a troubled uncertainty in her heart, an annoying grating brought on by Elise's revelation. It didn't seem right for a father to choose a husband for his daughter, then die and leave her bound to his wishes. She'd read of this in other cultures, but in *America. . . ?*

One by one the children came, unburdening satchels and lunch pails. Some of them Elise greeted with a cheery salutation; some she patted on the shoulder. All were made to feel special.

For the community, Elise's departure would be a great loss. She would be remembered, however short her tenure. Henry Harris used to say it wasn't the quantity of time one had but the quality.

The bell rang; the children were seated. "I have an idea!" beamed Elise. "Would you like to have a guest teacher today?" The pupils applauded.

"Would you agree to teach the classes, Mrs. Harris?" A roaring volume of hand clapping came from Amy's nieces and nephews.

"I'll be glad to give you a rest," Amy said. "Why don't you take the day off?"

"I could use the day," admitted Elise. "I need to make out report cards and put these cucumbers to pickle in alum and brine water. Thank you, Mrs. Harris." She picked up her grade book, the flour sack, her wide-brimmed hat, and slipped out.

Just before noon, Sarah discovered that Matilda had left her lunch box at home. Hank was plowing, and she was in the midst of making hominy. She had already applied the lye and couldn't leave her stirring. When Alan came through the door, she nabbed him.

"Alan, will you run to the school and take Tilly's lunch?" she pleaded. "She forgot it, and I'm busier than a cutworm on a tomato plant."

"Be glad to. I'll run by home and change my shirt."

"You look okay."

"Not for the eyes of twenty students, Sarah. I represent the government of Texas, remember."

When he went to make himself presentable, he told his mother, "Sarah forgot to send Matilda's lunch this morning. I'm going to take it to her and may stay to do some observing. It'll help on my next report in Austin."

Scarcely had his shadow left the front door when Martha ran to find Sally. "Sally! Alan is goin' t' th' school. He'll meet Elise Young in person . . . an' mayhap he'll be marriage-bitten!"

"That's good news, Mama, but try not to get your hopes up. Alan is crowding thirty, and he has a mind of his own. I'm certain he won't be pushed into anything he doesn't choose himself."

"All I've ever asked is a chance fer him t' be with her, Sally-girl. Fer that's all it will take."

"Seems you've got your single wish, Mama."

"An' I've been a-couplin' that wish with prayer."

However, when Alan entered the schoolroom, it was Amy who greeted him instead of Elise. "Come along in,

Alan, and meet the pupils," she said. "We've given the regular teacher a day off, and we'll put you on the program for today if you'll stay awhile."

Alan smiled and nodded.

"Students, this is Mr. Alan Harris from the capitol of our state." More hand clapping followed Amy's announcement.

"Alan, why don't you tell the class something about your work at the capitol."

Alan simplified his job description then told them about the governing body, the laws in the making, and the capitol building itself. He presented the information at an easy, enjoyable pace.

"And what, exactly, are your aspirations for our school system, Mr. Harris?" prompted Amy.

"First, I would like to see equal educational opportunities for all races, all social classes, all ages. Second, I want all teachers to receive a proper wage. Third, we need to place better teaching tools in the hands of our educators."

"And you are particularly concerned with country schools?"

"Right," said Alan. "Perhaps because I'm a farm boy. I like to look into the years to come and see the awesome possibilities. Now that the horseless carriage has proven trustworthy, I foresee a time when such carriages may be sent to outlying areas and transport rural children to a central school somewhere."

"That's very interesting, Mr. Harris."

He grinned at Amy. "A good platform, huh?" She nodded, and he continued. "I'd like to see special grants of money or scholarship programs that would open doors to higher education for anyone who wished to avail himself or herself of it."

"Are schools your primary area of interest?"

"Yes, but not my only interest. I want health care for all sick people whether or not they have money. My brother is a doctor, and although I do not agree with all his projections for the future in the medical field, I do want to see a better health plan. I want to see a day when we can all work together to assist our indigent aged, our underprivileged society. It won't come easy. Indeed, it will come as a great sacrifice to many of us, and some of the laws will doubtless be abused. But," he tossed out his hands, "I want everyone to have a fair chance in life."

The room filled with a rumble of fresh acclaim.

"I have a brother who is a preacher, one who is a rancher, one who is a smithy, and one who is a carpenter. Each of us has our own unique talents given by God, none more important than the other or better than another. But working together as a team in harmony with each other and our heavenly Father, we can reach our greatest potential."

The students like it.

"Thank you, Mr. Harris," Amy said. "I wish that Miss Young could have been here to hear you."

Alan left to walk toward the bridge, thinking how swiftly time had passed and how soon he must return to the fast-paced life in Austin. He almost dreaded it after these few days of peace and fellowship with the ones he loved.

Austin. Dismal apartment buildings. Processed food. Society's demands.

And Mr. Jorgensen's daughter. . . .

CHAPTER TWELVE

Unfortunate Travelers

Earl Taylor was as close to the brink of despair as ever a man had come without falling in. A stubble of a beard, four days old, worried his thin face. Ghosts of fear and uncertainty swarmed around him.

His wife and four grandchildren sat in the broken-down wagon, their stomachs empty since daybreak. Now the sun was past its peak and headed toward the west. Last night's supper had consisted of a handful of early summer grapes. The youngest child, only a few weeks old, had started fretting hours ago, smacking at his tiny fists.

Trying to remain near the river, Mr. Taylor had missed the road somewhere. Now a wheel had gone bad on the buggy. He pulled off his wash-faded shirt and used it for a seine in hopes of catching a fish that he could broil on a bed of coals for the family's nourishment.

He shook his head to rid himself of thoughts that scratched and hurt. His wife, Eva, hadn't wanted to make the trip at all. She wasn't well. But there were other reasons, too. She had never forgiven her wayward daughter for running away with an irresponsible kid of a man twice her age and half her intelligence. Then she'd birthed a daughter too soon. Two boys followed in rapid succession; there had been a five-year gap between them and the last child.

They hadn't seen the girl since she left home and had scarcely heard from her over the years. She lived her own untamed life, following untamed men.

When the telegram came that his daughter was desperately ill, Earl made plans to go to her, but Eva balked. Why should she go running to a girl who had given her nothing but heartache? But when Earl threatened to leave Eva behind, she acquiesced. Rather than stay at home alone, she went along. Now Earl was glad she'd come and didn't know what he would have done with the children had she not made the trip to the high plains with him. She had her unwilling hands full, he admitted to himself, and she was growing weaker. If only he could make it home!

Upon their arrival in Seminole, their daughter had gone on to her questionable destination in the hereafter and her "husband" was nowhere to be found. A harried neighbor, with a brood of seven under her own wings, sheltered the Taylors' four grandchildren, awaiting the hoped-for appearance of the grandparents of the orphans. She shooed the Taylors away with hardly a civil word, and in his haste, Mr. Taylor forgot to check the wagon's soundness before starting back east.

He thought they would surely be home by now, but since he had missed the road some miles back, Earl didn't know how far they might be from their native county of Navarro. At least, according to the sun, they were still going in the right direction. The journey had stretched over many days, and if his calculations were right, this must be Good Friday. What a paradox.

His present concerns were food, the repair of the broken wheel—and a way to stop Eva's chronic complaining about the burden of the children.

Her agitated voice reached him now. "Earl!"

"Just a minute, Eva." He netted the fish that swam upstream, hoping the threadbare shirt would hold. Susan, the oldest of his grandchildren, stood watching him mutely. She pointed toward the buggy.

"I'm coming," he called a bit sharply as he slid the end of a small forked stick through the fish's gills and pulled the wet shirt across his bare shoulders. "Here. Hold the fish until I get back." He handed the stick to the girl.

"What do you want, Eva?" He pushed his head of unkempt hair into the buggy.

"This baby's a-dying, Earl. He won't live the day out. And what'll we do with his body? We haven't the money for a proper burial and no way to get to an undertaker. Will we just drop him in the river?"

"I'm doing the best I know how to do, Eva." His voice was tired, his patience taxed too long. "The rest is up to the Almighty. If He wills that the child should live, then he will. If not, he won't."

"The woman that kept him said he has been poorly since his birthing. She warned me that we'd likely never make it back to our farm with him. You can't blame me if he dies, Earl—"

"Nobody's blaming you for anything, Eva. It just seems that Providence has laid a mighty hard and crusty hand on this old grandpa." He turned to walk away, his shoulders drooped with hopelessness. "I caught a little fish. If I can get a fire started, I'll cook it for you and the children."

"Feed Oscar and Rufus," she said. "They're the only ones not a'ready ailing. Keep them well at least."

A twig snapped, bringing Mr. Taylor's head up with a jerk. The sound sent Susan skittering away like a scared animal. Alan stepped into the clearing.

"I beg your pardon for disturbing your picnic," he said.

The man rubbed his prickly chin. "I'm . . . not trespassing on somebody's private property, am I?"

Alan smiled. "The river is free."

"You wouldn't happen to have a match, would you, young man?"

"Not with me, but I can get you one. That is—it isn't for a smoke, is it? I'm afraid my conscience wouldn't let me be an accomplice for a tobacco habit."

"No. I don't smoke. I'm—I'm just trying to cook a—a fish for my grandsons." He jerked his head toward the buggy, shaded by a giant cottonwood tree scarred by an old lightning injury. Susan peeked from behind the broken buggy wheel.

"Troubles?" Alan asked.

"Akin to Job," Mr. Taylor looked at the toes of his worn boots. "Serious, I'm afraid. I—I'm down on my luck. Sometimes even a man wants to sit down and cry. Started home from the Caprock and ran out of food . . . money . . . sick baby . . ." The words seemed to snag on something in the man's throat. "My paw said bad fortune comes in pounds, good fortune in ounces. Since I left home, I haven't seen an ounce of good fortune."

"Why don't you bring your family up to the house?" Alan suggested. "Mama will be glad to fix them a good, hot meal."

"I . . . I don't know if I could get Eva—that's my wife —to anybody's place. She's shy and not very agreeable right now. Not a whit well herself. See, she didn't want to make this trip in the first place, and now that everything's gone sour, I'm afraid she's blaming me. She was never handy with children, even in her well days, and we're left with these grandchildren since my daughter's untimely death . . ." Every word inflicted more pain.

"If you'll wait right here, Mr.—?"

"Taylor. Earl Taylor."

"My name is Alan Harris, and I will get you some help."

Mr. Taylor made a bitter sound that loosely resembled a laugh. "Yes, I suppose I'll wait. Do you have any idea what else a man in my position could do but wait? I'm stranded."

"Where is your home, Mr. Taylor?"

"I wish I knew. Somewhere east of here. I don't know how far it is map wise. We don't live in no town in particular. I guess Milford would be the closest. That's where we go to buy chicken feed."

"We'll get you fixed up and on your way, sir. I'm glad you broke down near enough that we could help. My brother, William, is a smithy and knows all about buggies and wheels." He turned to go.

Mr. Taylor's face lost some of its tautness. He headed for the vehicle, the fatigue he suffered showing in the way he threw his feet in front of him when he walked.

Alan found William's wife in Martha's kitchen

kneading bread. "I need you, Nellie, and quickly," he said. "There's a woman and some hungry children down by the river. Their buggy is broken down. Bring some biscuits and ham and anything else you can find."

"A woman travelling alone with her children?" Nellie dusted her flour-whitened hands on her apron and reached for a sack. "Who is she? Where is she from? Where is she going?"

Alan laughed. "I didn't ask her to fill out a questionnaire. But no, she isn't alone. Her husband is with her. Their name is Taylor, and the poor man is about to the end of his tether. He caught one tiny bream to feed the whole family! How he caught that one, I don't know. His shirt is soaked; I guess he jumped in after it. Where's William? We have a buggy wheel that needs repairing so they can be on their way."

"He took Mama Harris to the Springs for some supplies. They should be back any time now. There are extra wheels in Hank's barn. Leave William a note, and we'll go on."

Nellie threw the breakfast leftovers into the sack. "How many of them are there?"

"I don't know. I saw one girl, maybe eight or ten years old, peeking from behind the buggy. She was a little smaller than Matilda. A couple of boys that looked like twins were padding around in the shallow water. And the man mentioned a sick baby. I'm a bit confused as to how they ended up here. Apparently, they missed their road somewhere. I don't know how long it's been since they've had any food—"

"Why didn't you just bring them to the house, Alan? It would have been faster and more convenient. Was the man afraid to leave his buggy? I'm sure no one would bother anything."

"He said his wife was people shy and out of sorts. I couldn't get them to budge."

Nellie, Alan's favorite sister-in-law, straightened her six-foot frame resolutely and looked at him. "Then we'll go to them."

CHAPTER THIRTEEN

A Frightened Doctor

Nellie wove a story from the fabric of the scene she saw, sized up the situation, and didn't like the size of it. The despair in Mrs. Taylor's eyes, her sallow complexion, and the baby's hardly audible cry told their tale well. This family had suffered deprivation for much too long. She hoped there wouldn't be a death plot in the story somewhere.

One look told Nellie that Eva Taylor had once been a large woman. Now she was wasted. Giving witness to this fact were bags of loose skin that sought for a place to fit and look right. Her hair was stringy, dried by too much wind. She was a picture of poor health.

At first, Eva would not communicate with Nellie, but the younger woman had a way with people. When she offered the food she had brought, the woman's dull eyes showed a thread of hope.

The boys dived out of the water and came sloshing and dripping at the grandmother's beck. The oldest child, a girl, slid down the side of the buggy out of sight and reached a dirty hand around for bread.

After they had eaten, Nellie began her gentle manipulation of the unresponsive woman. "You must be very tired, Mrs. Taylor," she said. "My brother-in-law said you have been through a great misfortune. Life can be a bumpy road. I offer you my sympathy. How long have you been journeying?"

"Too long," was the terse reply.

"Alan said you had missed your road."

"We was trying to stay by the river so's I could wash the baby's dirty diapers with river water."

"Would you like for me to hold the baby and let your arms rest awhile?"

Pent up emotions contorted her face. "Do you know anything about babies, missus?"

"I . . . I've never had any of my own—though I've yearned for children for years. I've helped my sister with hers. . . ."

"Have you ever seen a baby die?" The words staggered about drunkenly. Something in her eyes—eyes that were small, dark and lusterless—made Nellie prickle all over with needles of dread.

"Yes." Nellie tried to keep her voice even. "My sister's first baby died. That's been several years ago."

"I think this one's a-dying." She pulled back the dingy wrap, exposing a tiny skeleton.

Nellie stifled a gasp. "Is—has he—she been ill long?"

"It's a boy child. I guess he's been ailing all his life. Nothing will stay with his innerds. He's skinny as a starved crow. He may be one of them liver-bound babies. There's no hope for them."

"But—"

"Earl and me don't know what to do if he up and dies along the way. Just dig him a grave with our own hands, I guess. Better it would have been if he had gone when his mother did." She paused and looked away. "But not *where*," she added quickly.

"What is the baby's name?"

"I don't think he's got none. The woman that kept him since my daughter's death didn't think he had been titled. But what's the use in naming a baby that don't plan to stay around long nohow? Let God give him a name up there." She looked up.

"Surely there's something that can be done. We have to try."

"We wouldn't know where to find a doctor even if we had the money and the buggy was fixed so's we could leave right now."

Nellie's mind grabbed, pulled toward a solution. She almost laughed when it came to her so plainly. "My brother-in-law is a doctor, Mrs. Taylor. And a good one! He is visiting now. I'll take the baby to him if you'd like."

"Please!" She almost threw the listless infant, cover and all, into Nellie's arms.

"Would you like to come with me, Mrs. Taylor, and meet the doctor for yourself?"

"Thank you, no. I have these others here to see after. And I never feel comfortable at someone else's place. When I get nervous, I take terrible stomach gases."

"Then please understand that we'll do our best." Nellie fled with her featherweight cargo toward Sally's cottage where Chester lodged. She'd never seen a baby so emaciated.

She heard William whistling before she saw him

rolling a wheel down the arched-over footpath. The disconnected tatters of song he warbled eventually fell into a meaningful tune. Nellie recognized the song as "He Cares for the Sparrow."

"And are you not worth more than many sparrows?" she whispered to the child in her arms.

She stepped aside to let William pass and clipped out the words, "Very ill baby. I'm taking him to Chester. Pray." Then she hurried on headlong.

Chester took one look and said he doubted they could save the nameless boy. He was too far gone. "If only we could have gotten him sooner. Even a day sooner would have made a difference," he fretted. "He is dehydrated to nothing."

But Nellie ignored his prognosis, rocking and singing and crooning as Chester shot orders to Sally for supplies. Thin applesauce and buttermilk for the wretched diarrhea. That might induce the stomach processes to go back to work. Weak blackberry syrup. Sterilized water. "A part of it depends on how much fight he has left," he said, mopping his brow. "I don't know how he's fought this long."

"Don't give up, little one," Nellie urged, kissing the bit of brownish down on the tiny head. If this baby died, it would mean one less child in the world when for more than a decade Nellie had asked God for one more—and that it be hers.

"Sally, go get Mama," Chester barked. "I need to send her to the river with a message for the grandmother."

Martha came on the run, splatters of whey still on her face from turning the clabber into the cottage cheese cloths to be hung on the clothesline to drip.

"Mama, we have a very sick baby here. Belongs to some people broken down by the river—"

"I saw Alan's note."

"Their name is Taylor," added Nellie.

"What can I do?"

"Go tell Mrs. Taylor," Chester continued, "that I'll need to keep the baby here until morning. I don't want her to get any false hopes, though. The chances are not favorable that the little one will still be alive when daylight breaks."

"I'd hate like ever'thing to tell a poor mother that, Chester!"

"She's not the mother; she's the grandmother," Nellie interrupted.

"That might be worser."

"She knows."

"All th' same—"

"She's not expecting the baby to live, Mama."

"Well, I s'pose we can bury it with ourn; Henry won't mind. He was always big-hearted. On th' great resurrectin' mornin', it won't matter where nobody is nohow. God can find us an' sort us."

"And tell her," Chester said, "that she'll probably want to come up here and sit the night in case the end comes."

"I'm not sure she'd be comfortable leaving the other children, Chester," spoke up Nellie. "Let her know, Mama, that if she can't come, I'll sit the night and care for the baby as if he were my very own."

"And be sure to tell her there'll be no charges," finished Chester. "Not a dime."

113

"I hope my rememberer can hold all this in its lap," Martha said.

When Martha had gone, Chester turned to Nellie. "If we can ward off the death angel tonight, we might have a chance."

"Why are nights so much worse, Chester?"

"I've wondered that myself, Nellie." He looked tired and much older than his almost thirty years. "But this is one night I dread. If I lose, it will be my first . . . loss. This is when being a doctor is frightening."

CHAPTER FOURTEEN

Helen's Decision

Claire ordered a bowl of chowder, but Helen said she wasn't hungry.

"Are you still pining for Mr. Dreamboat?" Claire chided. She didn't wait for an answer. "Have you heard from him?"

"No." Helen cut her short. "I posted him a card to his mother's address. He should have gotten it by now. I asked that he call, and I've sat by the phone for *hours*."

"A watched pot never boils, Helen. Wasn't it Socrates who said that?" She giggled.

"No, it was Plato."

"Do something to move time. Take a trip to the coast. Throw a party. Go out with some of your other swains. You have a pile of broken hearts to pick from. I've never known you to sit and wait for a telephone to ring."

"You're forgetting, Claire, that I'm going to marry Alan Harris—and no one else. There's the difference. When one is in love—is heart-committed—one waits."

"Have you considered that he might have a sweetheart back home?"

"I'm not given to negative thoughts. My father taught me better. Alan specified that he was going to visit his family. He's much too polished to marry a country laundress or kitchen maid. He was born to grace higher circles, and I give him the benefit of knowing that. He will require someone prestigious."

"You."

"Me."

"So you've been sitting at home with your hands folded since the day he left?"

"Have my hands ever been folded? I've investigated every facet of Alan Harris's life so that I may be prepared to share his thoughts, plans, ideals."

"You *have* changed."

"I'm glad you've noticed at last."

"And it becomes you to think of someone besides yourself."

"If that was meant to be a compliment, thanks."

"But tell me about your detective work."

"I started at his boardinghouse. And what a wretched place it is for a prince! Common as a winter cold. On an off street. On his salary, I'm sure he could do much better. I don't know what to make of it."

"You wouldn't be willing to live with him there?"

"Heavens, no! Father wouldn't hear of it. And that's what set my mind to working on a plan. I spoke to Father about fixing up the south dormer room upstairs for rent. It's private with an outside staircase. It would be a perfect place for Alan—until we are married."

"Did your father agree?"

"Father doesn't know my motives—my design—yet, but he will be pleased. He never denies me anything. With

Alan right on the property, he and Alan could work together evenings."

"Then?"

"Then I questioned Father about Alan's work. Father
is overjoyed that I've taken an interest in the school
reform bill. He said I was maturing."

"What did you learn?"

"Alan wants a guaranteed wage for all teachers while
Father wants mandatory attendance laws in the state of
Texas for all children from age seven to sixteen. They
are also politicking for another grade to be added, from
eleven to twelve. Both of them want required subjects
in each classroom and an improved grading system. I
didn't know legislation could be so fascinating."

Claire shook her head in disbelief. "I can't imagine
you, Helen Jane Jorgensen, being concerned with anything but the next ball and what you are going to wear."

"When you're in *love*, Claire, *everything* changes. Now
I have to be worried about groomsmen, a wedding gown,
a reception cake, and invitations."

"I've never been there, so I shouldn't know."

"Love will make you do a lot of strange things. You'll
be more amazed when you hear me out."

"Amaze me, please."

"I went to Alan's church last Sunday." She lowered
her voice to a hushed undertone. "That was the biggest
shock of all. But, Claire, Mother must *never* know that
I went; she'd be mortified and would put a squelch on all
my plans."

"How . . . how did you manage to go without her
knowing?"

"I pretended to be ill, waited until she left for the

117

Avenue Church, then slipped out. Father was away on a weekend golfing trip."

"You didn't!"

"I hated to deceive them, but I had to know—"

"You can say penance later. What was it like?"

"The building was a dreadful excuse for a sanctuary. Nothing at all like our cathedral. No belfry or stained glass or carved pews. It was, indeed, a shabby storefront structure bordering slumhood with naked floors and patches of plaster missing from the ceiling. I snagged my silk stockings on a splintery old bench!"

Claire's curiosity was wide awake. "But the people, the religion—was it very much the same as ours?"

"Most of the people were poor peasants. They dressed plain, nothing fancy. Some looked as though they had come in their work clothes. Their simplicity made me feel like a—like a hypocrite—or maybe even a *sinner*. At first, I couldn't even picture Alan there. Then it all seemed right for him. The people were real . . . and so is Alan."

"Is their liturgy so different?"

"Claire, it was like nothing I've ever attended before. No one waited for the other to say a prayer or read one. They didn't even take turns. They all prayed together and aloud! There was no pipe organ, just a man strumming a Spanish guitar, and they sang without the benefit of note sheets. And most clapped their hands in rhythm to the music! At the leader's invitation, each of them jumped up and gave a bit of an autobiography and told how their lives had been changed. It was a volunteer thing. Some of them talked out during the sermon, saying amen and hallelujah. The building was a-roar with noise, but nobody seemed to notice or care."

118

"So you excused yourself and left?"

"I couldn't."

"They locked you in?"

"No, it was as if something—some spirit, some un-seen hand—compelled me to stay. I . . . felt something I've never felt before. It was almost frightening, like I wanted to laugh and cry at the same time. It felt good. A sort of magnet kept pulling me toward the front. I had to hold on to the bench to keep from running and kneel-ing at what they called a mourner's bench. I felt sorry for every bad thing I'd ever done. I guess I just got caught up in the drama of it all."

"Do they believe in, well, God and the Bible?"

"I think, Claire, that they understand the Bible in a deeper, more personal way than our shallow theological professors."

"Helen!"

"What the preacher said made so much sense. I went there to observe, maybe even to criticize, but I got a . . . revelation."

"*YOU*, Helen?"

"Yes. I had never given much thought to God or eter-nity, but when I did I had my own mental diagram of God's order. God, the Father, was Lord over the heavens: the sun and moon and stars. When the lightning fright-ened me, He was the Lord to whom I should appeal.

"Then the second person was Jesus. Since He once lived here on earth, He would be the one to take care of the everyday things I needed in life. I've never lacked for much, so He wasn't very busy on my behalf.

"Then the third God, the Holy Ghost, seemed to be responsible for the unseen things—germs and death and maybe my soul. Each Lord had His own throne with the Father occupying the biggest—"

"You know our rector told us not to try to figure all this out." The set of Claire's mouth suggested she'd rather tiptoe past a discussion of the Deity. "It's beyond human comprehension and too deep for us anyhow. Leave all that to the prophets and sages. I'm—"

"No, Claire, listen. We've made it hard. It's so simple, so elementary. Alan's preacher called it a 'truth,' and now I can see it as clear as a bell. When the man read a passage of Scripture about Jesus having control over the winds and the sea, I said to myself, 'Wait a minute! Jesus is getting into God's territory.' "

"Now you're getting *me* mixed up, Helen."

"I'll unmix you. It's plain as daylight. God is a *Spirit*, has always been a Spirit. He is everywhere and can go everywhere. He can appear in any form He pleases: a burning bush, a rock in a wilderness, an angel. He's here now—"

Claire shuddered as she stared into her bowl of soup gone cold.

"But God made Himself a body and came down to earth in human form. Now God has a face and a name. God was *in Christ* reconciling the world unto Himself. Christ was God come to earth to be with us. Can't you see, Claire? There's only one Lord."

"What about . . . about the third person?"

"The Holy Spirit isn't a separate person either. The Spirit fell on the believers on the Day of Pentecost. That wasn't a third person that fell upon the 120 in the upper room; that was the Spirit of the one God. Claire, there aren't three persons. The throne John saw in the last book of the Bible was for Jesus, our Lord and our God."

"I'd never thought about it, really."

"We've never taken the time, you and I. But I cannot deny the truth that I came face to face with at Alan's church."

"So you joined Alan's church?"

Helen leaned forward. "It's not a church you can join, Claire. It's an experience. Their baptism is not even for church membership; it's for the taking away of your sins, and it's done in the name of Jesus. They call it being 'born again' of the water and of the Spirit. I've read the second chapter of Acts at least ten times while I've sat by the phone. The preacher was right; it's all right there. They're going by the pattern of the first and original church. And I'm afraid ours has strayed far away."

"Did you get . . . born again?"

"No. I knew I could never make so drastic a change. Mother would disown me."

"So what will you do?"

"I'll go to my church on the avenue and let Alan go to his."

"Even if he wishes you to go with him?"

"I won't try to change Alan, and he won't try to change me. I doubt if we'd be successful even if we tried. Alan's faith is strong. If I could convert him to my church, I don't think I'd wish to. His uniqueness is one reason I admire him. He's not your average self-seeking, materialistic Romeo. And I'm thinking his religion is what sets him above the others."

"What about your children? Wouldn't they feel pulled apart?"

"Do I feel pulled apart? My mother and father go to

different churches, and I've never found it to be a problem."

"But religion . . . that's a mainmast in a home. Your mother's and father's views are not so diametrically opposed."

"I've given it a lot of thought, and I don't see that it will pose any difficulty."

"But what if Alan doesn't agree with your philosophy? You remember what that Molly said about them not marrying outside their beliefs."

There was silence. "No," Helen repeated, "religion won't be a factor. I won't *let* it be."

CHAPTER FIFTEEN

The Warning Flag

Martha and Eva Taylor struck up a chord of empathic kinship, finding their lower notes written on the same scale. Layer by layer the distrust peeled off, leaving a thin skin of friendship.

"My son, th' doctor, sent word that he needs t' keep th' baby fer th' night," Martha relayed. "Mayhap he'll live an' mayhap he won't. He said not to make no hopes. He said you could come an' sit ifn you wanted. My daughter-in-law, Nellie, said she'd sit in fer you ifn you couldn't come."

"I've got these others here, Miz Harris—"

"Jest 'Marthy' me."

"—and we have our bedrolls tied on back. The boys, they're a handful all by theirselves, so near the same age and all. Earl and me are really too old and ailing to care for the kids, but their pa couldn't be rounded up nowhere. It fell our unwelcome lot to take them. They're a big responsibility."

"My sorry is fer you, Miz Taylor."

"I'm Eva."

Martha handed her new friend an understanding smile. "I know 'bout responsibility. I had nine, an' a tenth is in yon graveyard. I would'a got the jeebies fierce just thinkin' o' takin' them t' anybody's house. We ain't askin' you t' make yerself nervous-sick. I'll jest send someone with some more grub fer you t' eat afore dark."

"You're too . . . merciful."

"Ifn 'twas me broke down an' with a sick-nigh-death baby, I'd hope to break down close to some mercious family."

Martha's sixth sense told her that the woman needed to unburden her soul to rid herself of some plague that ate away at her peace of mind.

"An' I know how it'll make you feel t' see th' dirt go over a grandlad. It happened to me, only it was a bit of a girl. Most nigh stopped th' beatin' o' my heart. You got only boys here?"

A sudden pain made Eva's eyes darken, "No. The first was a girl." She looked around with a certain caution. "She's a-hiding somewhere. She moves about like a ghost in the night. Gives me a smothery feeling sometimes to watch her." Then she added, almost in a whisper. "She ain't *right*. She's *afflicted*."

"How like?" Martha pressed.

"She can't talk. Nary a word. Can't even say her own name, which is Susan. Rufus and Oscar said she used to make noises, but I don't put much stock in their stories. Rufus and Oscar are her brothers—or half-brothers." She bunched her shoulders. "They're six and seven and are named for my pa and for Earl's pa. Anyways, they said the woman that kept Susan until we got there told her if she couldn't stop jabbering and talk plain like everybody else, then to just shut up. She must have punished Susan pretty bad. The boys say she hasn't made another sound from that day to this."

"Have you had her t' ery a doctor?"

"Oh, no!" Eva laid her hand over her mouth then took it away. "She's one of those *sin* babies. The kind that their ma marks before they're ever born. Then they come along into the world as a punishment. Most is evil possessed, I've been told. But I haven't noticed this one being mean. Or vengeful. Or even trying to harm herself. Not that I can tell, anyway."

"Eva, I—"

"You see, my daughter, Mattie, was wild and wayward. We put a lot of hopes on her, her being our onliest one, but she had her own mind and it wasn't a clean mind, it grieves me to say. I tried to teach her to sew and tat and crochet like a young lady should, but she wanted rather to run like the wind or climb trees. She . . . she went after wild men when she got older. A bad one came along and she got into trouble and run off with him. From that day to this, she never came home.

"I don't know as she ever married the man she left with. He skipped on her and Mattie put the Taylor name on Susan. Then she married a traveling man. The boy's last names is Adams. They came along back to back and are both same fathered. You can tell it, they look so much alike. Mattie writ in a letter that they looked just like their pa.

"Then that one deserted her off on the high plains at a place called Seminole. She had one more man after that, but I don't even know the name of that one. That was the baby's pa.

125

"Over the years, we only heard from Mattie now and then when she or one of the children got real bad sick.

"Now you know why Susan is like she is," she finished.

"I used t' b'lieve th' same way you do 'bout marred children, Eva. But I found in the Good Book where God don't visit th' fathers' sins—or th' mothers'—on innocent little children. That wouldn't seem fair ifn He did, would it?"

"I never knew that was in the Bible."

"Jest listenin' t' yer story, I'd say you've got t' do somethin' that might be a mite hard now but will be easy in th' end."

"What be that?"

"You gotta fergive yer daughter. She's gone now, but you can ask God to release you from yore feelin's. Holdin' bad feelin's won't do nuthin' but eat away at yer own soul. Ifn you can't find it in yer heart to do it single-handed, ask God fer His almighty help."

"I do want to be right at judgment."

"Ifn I might borrey yer ear, I'd like to tell you my own parable. It might help you. I b'lieved th' sin an' shame punishment jest like you do. Only worser. I carried that idea fer many a year. It almost sent my soul an' body to th' burnin' place. You see, my husband had an unperfect niece cast upon us unwanted. I treated her shamefully, I'm sorry t' admit. Worser'n a dog. But God had to strip me down t' my very gizzard.

"My own baby girl got in a fire an' that lovely crippled-up girl saved my Sally's life. She returned good fer all my evil. Then I saw it was *me* what had th' bad spirit instead of her.

126

"Crippled an' deef an' dumb an' blind ain't always th' work o' an evil spirit or th' bogey man. I found out that th' afflicted child God sent into our lives was a *bent-winged angel* who got her wings bent up in th' trip to us. She stayed fer a few years longer—t' make th' world a better place—" Martha choked up, using her apron to wipe her tears, "then she left us."

Eva started to cry. "I guess Susan can't help what her ma did, can she? But why does *she* have to suffer, Martha?"

"Only God holds that answer, an' it's naught o' our business t' question."

"I wonder what will happen to Susan when I'm gone on." Eva laced and unlaced her fingers. "I know I'm not going to live long. Probably someone will put her away in the asylum."

"Now, Eva, let me give you a pure truth. God takes care of His bent-winged angels. You don't give it no fret. I was a mind to put Henry's niece there, but God put up roadblocks. He'll send somebody along t' take up where you leave off ifn you ask Him."

"Martha, I'm beholden to you. I—I think I know what I have to do. I think God is showing me right now." She pulled her sagging shoulders up. "You've been a big help. You've been more than generous. If I could ask just one small favor more of your doctor son—"

"Ask anything."

"Will you take Susan to him and have him to take a look at her leg? She has a wretched boil on the back side of her knee."

"Chester'll be more'n glad to tend her. He likes workin' with ailin' children. An' he said remind you there'd be no charges—now er ever.''

"Just a thank you don't seem enough.''

"He needs somethin' to fill up his lackin' hours. He lives up in Fort Worth an' he's come home fer a reunion. His wife stayed herself a'home. So he gets mighty lonesome an' fidgety an' restless. This'll occupy him.''

Eva Taylor called to Susan, but the child didn't come. "She's a-hiding,'' the weary woman sighed. "She's scared of folks. But I guess she's a right to be, from what the boys tell. She's been knocked around. I'll have to fetch her.''

As Martha waited, she watched her sons work on the buggy wheel. Alan smiled up at her. "We've almost got it,'' he said. "But we need to check the other wheels, too. This coach will be ready to roll by morning.''

He's so much like Henry, Martha thought, *yet so unlike him*. Easy-going. Personable. Helpful. Always anxious to make the world a better place for someone else. But Henry had never been as quick, as lissome.

Eva returned with a terrified Susan in tow. But Martha Harris hadn't mothered ten children without an uncanny knack for understanding them. "Come, Susan,'' she said with a soft huskiness. "Mayhap you'll get t' see my granddaughter, Tilly, an' her kitty cat. Tilly's jest yore age, an' her cat's name is Scaredy-cat. Scaredy-cat has four furry babies an' all you have t' do is hold 'um close so's they won't fret of fallin'.''

Martha won. Susan took her hand and managed a near smile. The two started up the hill toward the house.

When Martha turned to wave to Eva Taylor, her eyes caught on a small object. Below them, in a private cul-de-sac of the thicket, which provided a wooded hiding place from all directions, a small patch of cloth clung to a thorn, waving like a shrunken flag.

A warning flag.

It was a piece of checked gingham, red and white. *From Molly's dress.* She'd been to the river to meet Alan!

For the rest of the way home, Martha was as mute as the child whose hand she held.

CHAPTER SIXTEEN

Claire's Gleanings

Helen pulled Claire into the Jorgensens' library, where the floor was pampered with Persian rugs and a massive brass eagle looked down on them from the mantel. Claire had called to say that she had some startling information she'd gathered from her Uncle Randolph, and when Helen learned that Claire's gleanings concerned Alan, she insisted that her friend come over at once.

"What is it, Claire? Tell me!"

"Mum's brother is in town for a medical convention. He's staying at our house. He knows Alan's twin brother."

"The doctor from Fort Worth?"

"Yes. My Uncle Randolph."

"Knows Chester Harris?"

"Better than that. Chester Harris married his stepdaughter, Candice. It was almost an accident that I found out."

"Claire!"

"Do you want to hear the whole story?"

"Don't leave out one word!"

"Aunt Hortense had two children, Candice and John, when she married my uncle. Uncle Randolph agreed to pay for their education—whatever vocation they chose—when he wed Hortense. He never lacked for money and never had any children of his own. Candice thought she wanted to be a ballet dancer, then an actress, then a hair stylist, then I don't know what all. She jumped from one thing to another, never really following through with anything.

"Uncle Randolph, with a love for medicine, wanted John to go into the medical field, and John agreed. Uncle told him that's where the money is. John is a doctor now."

"And how did Candice meet Chester?"

"I'm coming to that part."

"Slowpoke."

"Chester came into Uncle Randolph's office one day with a burn on his foot from hot tar. He was working with a street crew in Fort Worth. Candice happened to be in the office that morning speaking with her stepfather when Chester got there. She liked his looks and friendliness and was between boyfriends at the time. She made an appointment for her father to check on his foot. His name and address were on the records. Her story is almost identical to yours, to hear Uncle tell it. It was love at first sight for Candice. After she saw Chester, all other men paled in his illustrious distinction."

"I can identify with her."

"Aunt Hortense pitched a fit. No daughter of hers, she howled, would marry a common laborer! She'd invested too much into her daughter to have her waste herself on a peon. She forbade Candice to see him, but Candice slipped around.

"In desperation, Auntie shipped men in from everywhere to take her daughter's attention from Chester, but it didn't work."

Helen hooted. "Good for Candice!"

"The more Hortense fought it, the more cunning Candice became in her schemes to meet Chester secretly.

"Candice is a foxy one; she's a bit older than Chester. At first, according to Uncle Randolph, Chester spurned her suggestions that they should marry. He pointed out that their backgrounds were painted on different canvases. But eventually she won."

"Your aunt finally agreed?"

"Not wholeheartedly. Candice appealed to Uncle Randolph, and when he saw that she had her heart set, he agreed to talk with Chester to see if they might bring Chester up to Hortense's standards. Together, Uncle and Candice convinced Chester that he would make a wonderful doctor, and Uncle offered to sponsor him through medical school. There was an agreement that when he finished the schooling, if he didn't like the profession, he wouldn't be held to it for a lifetime. Uncle says no one should have to be bound to a job he doesn't like. The choice would ultimately lie with Chester.

"By now Chester had fallen in love with Candice and didn't want to give her up. So he agreed to the arrangement.

"Aunt Hortense was afraid that he would go back on this truce of sorts, but he didn't. He enrolled in college the very next semester.

"When they married, none of his family came to the wedding. Knowing Hortense as I do, I can guess that it was a flamboyant affair with a reception at some fancy club—and with plenty of wine."

133

"She's happy with Chester now? Your aunt, I mean."

"Oh, very! She can't brag about him enough. He is working in the office with John, and Uncle claims he's by far the better doctor of the two. But Uncle says Hortense and Candice want him to have his own practice, even his own hospital. They have great ambitions for him. Uncle says he's an excellent children's doctor, but Candice wants him to be a heart surgeon. She says that's where all the research is concentrated and that's where the big bucks will be.

"And Candice has taken the strict religion right out of him, Helen! He was a zealot like Alan: no dances, no drinking, no cards. Uncle says she hasn't converted him to her kind of partying yet, but it's just a matter of time. Uncle says he's a very malleable sort, putty in Candice's hands."

"I wonder if he's just as nice. The changes that Candice insisted on didn't change his personality, did it?"

"Oh, lands, no! Uncle says he's even nicer. More sophisticated. More dedicated to his work and to Candice. He never crosses her. He even went to her church for a while, but now he says he doesn't have time to go anymore."

"That's great news, Claire. I must admit, I was a bit worried about Alan's religion after I visited his church. But if she can change Chester, I can change Alan!"

"Meeting Chester's family was quite a shock for Candice, Uncle said. She went to one of their family get-togethers the first year she and Chester were married. They are everything the black-haired girl said. How did she say it? *As country as cornpone in a black iron skillet.* They live in a comfortable enough house, but they still

have open prayers. All sorts of them. Mealtime prayers
and bedtime prayers and hello prayers and goodbye
prayers. One of the bunch is a preacher of sorts. When
they started speaking of God as if He were their personal
friend, Candice got antsy. And, too, Chester made the
mistake of taking her to his church. It was a crude wooden
affair with an uneducated parson as antiquated as the
building itself."

"Poor Candice."

"I think that's when she decided that those people
weren't of her world nor she of theirs. She has never been
back and says she will never go back in the future. However, she doesn't object to her husband going once a year.
He's there now."

"With Alan!"

"Yes."

"But you said it was almost by accident that you
learned about all this."

"I didn't make the connection until today. Candice
calls her husband Chess. I'd always heard Aunt Hortense
talking about 'Candice and Chess' and gave it no thought.
Then Uncle mentioned that Chess said he had a twin
brother who worked at the capitol building. That's when
the missing puzzle piece fell into place in my head. I'd
never heard Candice's last name and asked Uncle what
it was. He said Harris. Her husband is Dr. Chess Harris,
and his twin's name is Alan."

"Claire! Do you know what this means?"

"What?"

"When I marry Alan Harris, I'll almost be kin to you!"

"For a fact. You'll be the wife of my stepcousin-in-
law's brother."

Helen gave Claire an impulsive squeeze. "I know more than ever, Claire, that Alan Harris is the man I am destined to marry!"

A gleam of light from the window caught in the brass eagle's eye.

CHAPTER SEVENTEEN

The Forgotten Card

Sally's energy seemed inexhaustible. She melded the chain of chores so expertly that not a link was broken or missing. She gathered mountains of eggs and killed the hens for the family meals—pinfeathering, stuffing, trussing them.

Bending her back and bracing both feet, she turned the crank on the fussy separator. Henry always allowed that he had a "soft spot" for farm machinery, and the separator was one of his "investments." Sally marveled that the machine knew what to do when she poured fresh milk into the open top and watched milk come from one spout, cream from the other.

Martha was proud of her youngest. Every inch of her life was paved with good intentions. Her faults—if she had any—were all on the surface. She was as true as a taproot, that one.

Through the back door, Martha could see Sally's moist face now as she bowed over the washpot, prodding the clothes with the wooden plunger. Then she whittled more lye soap into the pot and stirred again, frowning her displeasure.

Martha opened the screen door and stepped out. Seeing the unhappy expression still on Sally's face, she scolded gently, "You're workin' too hard, Sally!"

"Not a bit of it, Mama." Sally looked up. "I like Papa's philosophy. He used to say he wanted to get the back of the job broken before midday. I'm trying to get the wash finished before the morning melts into afternoon. But there's something in this pot of clothes that I can't figure. Something is coming apart."

Martha looked at the floating debris. "Well, I can't imagine what 'twould be, Sally-girl. Somethin' white, ain't it? An' bitsy pieces swimmin' in there."

"You didn't leave anything in an apron pocket, did you, Mama?"

Martha looked blank. "No." Then her hand flew to her mouth in an expression of consternation. "Th' card!" she said with chagrin. "Oh, Sally, th' card!"

"Whatever are you talking about, Mama? You are as pale as warmed-over death. It can't be that bad."

"I forgot about it—"

"About what?"

"Alan's mail. Th' night of the sing when all of you were over t' Molly's, Miss Young brought a card fer Alan."

"Oh, Mama! You didn't tell me!"

"I fergot. But th' card is—" Martha took a dismal look into the churning water, "—gone."

"Elise's card is gone?"

"It wasn't from Elise."

"You just said Elise brought Alan a card."

138

"She did, but—"

"Either she did, or she didn't. Mama, you aren't making sense."

"Miss Young *delivered* th' card is what I meant to say."

"Personally?"

"Yes."

"I can't believe you forgot to give Alan a card from Elise—as hard as we've tried to stir up a romance."

"But you don't understand yet, Sally. Th' card was a mistake."

"A mistake? Now I *am* confused."

"Th' card got into Miss Young's post when it was really supposed t' have got into ourn. It got mixed with some o' her catalogues or somethin'. Th' backin' showed it to be fer Alan, so she brung it right over t' me t' give t' him—an' I—I fergot all about it—after I—I went t' have a talk with Myrt."

"What did Myrt have to do with the card?"

"Nothing, Sally."

"Then why is Myrt in the story at all?"

"Because my conversation with her made me disremember t' give Alan his card. When Myrt told me about Molly's husband bein' killed on his job an' how sorrowful Molly was an' all—"

Their eyes met, and a fire flashed in Sally's. "Don't believe everything you hear, Mama. Especially not from Molly's corner of the world." After an expensive tongue biting, she switched back to the subject of the card. "Suppose this shredded card was important to Alan. Have you any idea who or where it was from? It's evident we can tell nothing about it now."

"I did see th' name, though I wasn't bein' nosy. It was jest right there in plain sight—"

"Was it from his boss?"

"No, it was from a lady. Her name was Helen somethin-er-other. I can't remember th' other name now. It was a long, hard-to-say last name. Th' reason I recall th' Helen part is because that was my maw's sister's name. Aunt Helen."

"You didn't happen to see any of the message?"

"Th' last line—it sort of leaped out at me—sounded awful chummy." Her voice trembled. "Oh, Sally, I'm afeared he might have him a floosy off down in Austin."

"Now quit sniveling, Mama. And trust God a mite. That is almost good news to me. Most anybody would be better for Alan than Molly, with the kind of life she's lived!"

Martha thought back to the scrap of material clinging to the bush, a patch that could belong to no one but Myrt's wild granddaughter. "You're right, of course, Sally. Nuthin' in th' world could be much worser than that, could it?"

"And I think you'd best tell Alan about the card as soon as he comes in."

"He's still helpin' th' Taylors?"

"He and William found a bad axle. Chester's glad for more time."

"I'll be sure to tell him, Sally, th' first minute I get a chance." She left Sally to the wash and went back into the house, still berating herself.

It was dusk when Alan came in to usurp the wash basin. Martha stood behind him to hand him a clean towel for the roller.

140

"Alan," she said, sifting and straining her words, "I have some apologizin' to do."

"Don't come apologizing to me, Mama."

"Yes," Martha insisted, "I must—"

"Whatever it is, you're forgiven." He glanced up, water dripping from his chin.

"Th' night of th' sing at Myrt's, th' schoolteacher, Miss Young, brung you over a card that got tangled in with her mail. It was posted to you. I put it in my apron pocket against when you'd come home that evenin' an' I clean fergot t' give it t' you! It went in th' washpot t'day along with my apron, an' it's—mush."

"It likely wasn't important at any rate," Alan said. "You're too busy with taking care of this mob to be expected to have a perfect memory. Forget about it."

"But I'm afeared it *was* important, Alan."

"Did you notice where it was postmarked?"

"No, I didn't try t' look. But I did see a name at th' bottom. Th' name was Helen someone." She watched his face.

Something akin to alarm claimed his calm demeanor. "Helen *Jorgensen?*"

"I'd say on a stack of Bibles that that was it."

"Oh, Mama, I wish . . . I hope something hasn't happened. The card—may have something to do with my—my future."

Martha tried to interpret the disturbance of her son. The future he meant, she decided, was his marriage to the writer of the message. Else why would he be so distressed?

"I'll have to wire or call and let Helen know that I didn't get her letter. I could go into town, but the telegraph office will be closed now."

"You could use the horn here, Alan. It's cradled right there in th' front parlor where it's always been. Does this Helen lady have a telephone?"

"Yes, she does. And I guess I'd better do that, Mama, if you don't mind. When the bill comes in, send it to me, and I'll take care of it." He went to the telephone, but the party line was abuzz with a sharing of the day's gossip, and he had no desire to ask for the line and have the whole Brazos Point community listening in on his private conversation. "I'll try again later," he told Martha.

"I'm so sorry I let th' card get messed up, Alan," she grieved.

"Don't put your sorrow to it, dear Mama. I'll get it all straightened out, whatever the problem." He patted her shoulder.

As Martha lay in bed that night, she decided Alan had abandoned the idea of reaching this city woman. But quite late she heard a stir in the parlor and then heard him give the Austin number to the operator.

She pushed her nightcap back from her ears and strained to hear, propping herself on one elbow. For a long while Alan was quiet, and she supposed it took that much time for the connections to be completed. About the time he started to speak, the pump on the windmill went into noisy action, and she could only catch snatches of the one-sided conversation.

At first, she could only determine grunts of affirmative or negative monosyllables. Then there were partial sentences, most of which she couldn't decipher.

". . . We'll want a place of our own, of course. . . ."

The mill gave a raucous squawk outside, blotting out the next few words.

". . . I'll make the necessary arrangements . . . begin making plans as soon as I get back . . ."

". . . a short honeymoon . . ."

Martha didn't want to hear more. She pulled her cap back over her ears. "Oh, God," she cried, holding the feather tick pillow to her mouth so that no one could hear the fierce heart battle. "What I had feared has come upon me! My Alan—my pure, sweet Alan—is marryin' one of those cityfied heathens—an' there's not a blessed thing I can do about it! Would God he'd stay *single* th' rest of his days than it come to this! Oh, God, help me! Oh, Henry . . ."

Her faith evaporated while a shovel of discouragement dug the grave for her dying hopes.

CHAPTER EIGHTEEN

Troublesome Thoughts

The night was moonless. All nature held its breath as the frail, unnamed baby fought with the death angel.

For Nellie, demons of logic hopscotched between faith's angels, mocking and scoffing.

Worry . . . the demon.

Hope . . . the angel.

Fear . . . the demon.

Prayer . . . the angel.

Doubt . . . the demon.

Faith . . . the angel.

Despair . . . the demon.

Eventually, she learned to recognize swings of emotion, welcoming the angels, barring the door against the demons. If only Chester could hold the vultures of death at bay a while longer!

She felt as if she lived an eternity in that one long night. Her arms ached, and her eyes stung from lack of sleep, but when Chester said, "I think, with God's help, we're winning," tears of joy washed away the fatigue.

145

"But we need more time to be safe," the doctor continued. "If I can have just one more day with this gentleman, I'd say he'll have a fighting chance to live to be ninety."

Martha took over the care of Susan. She washed her hair in rain water, added vinegar to the rinse for sheen, then brushed her bronze hair into curls and tied it back with a colorful grosgrain ribbon. The effect was marvelous. Dressed in one of Matilda's hand-me-downs, the child underwent a moth-to-butterfly transformation. When she took the girl to Sally's cottage for a checkup on the festered leg, the smiling Susan held a wee kitten in her arms and looked as though she had stepped from the pages of a storybook.

"Why, she's—she's *beautiful*, Mama," whispered Sally. Mischief took over. "Almost as pretty as I was when I was her age!"

"An' she has a genius mind, Sally," Martha said. "One can 'most nigh tell what she wants t' say jest by lookin' at her eyes. Eva won't have no problems raisin' this'n. But how's th' bitsy one?"

"Better," Chester spoke up. "We need to keep him a while longer, though. I'm sure Mr. and Mrs. Taylor won't mind a few more hours' delay to save their grandson. One as fine as this one could win a war for our nation single-handedly. They can be proud of him."

"And Mama won't mind to feed the Taylors for the duration," Sally said. "She isn't happy unless she's taking care of somebody. You'd think she'd be wanting someone to take care of *her* after all these years."

"Stuff an' nonsense!" sputtered Martha. "I never could abide bein' idle. I'll take Susan back to her grandma an' tell them what you said—" Martha started, but Susan's eyes filled with tears, and she gave her head a vigorous shake, rearranging all the curls. She dropped the kitten and wrapped her arms around Nellie and the baby with an imploring gesture.

"She doesn't want to leave her baby brother," Nellie said. Then Susan went to encircle Martha with her embrace too. "And it seems, Mama Harris, that she doesn't want to leave you either."

"Send Alan," Chester said. "He's the one who found them. He'll be the personal representative to the Taylors from Harris headquarters."

"Mayhap we can git them t' come t' th' house—er at least closer," Martha said. "We could put food on th' big picnic table under th' backyard oak tree an' all have a grand time t'gether. Them boys would like that."

"Make it after school, and I'll invite Miss Young, Mama," Sally said.

Martha said nothing. Sally didn't know about the late-night telephone call. Why bother to tell her? Some miracle might transpire yet if Elise came.

"Who is Miss Young?" Chester wanted to know.

"The new schoolteacher. She came on at midterm when Mrs. Weathers's mother fell and broke her hip."

Chester turned his attention back to his work. "Probably Mrs. Taylor will want to see for herself how the baby is progressing—"

Alan himself came on a run that broke the thread of conversation. "Chester, your wife is on the telephone. She wants to speak with you. She said it is very important."

Like a spring, Chester bounced to his feet. "Thank you, Alan." He was out the door.

Sally looked after him. "Why doesn't Candice ever come with Chester to our reunions, Mama?"

"Candice is a higher class than we are, Sally. I'd say her roots prob'ly stretch all th' way to th' Order o' th' Garter."

"God made us all out of the same dust," argued Sally. "Dust we are and to dust we shall return."

"Yes, but there's city dust and country dust," grinned Alan. "Some dust has more ore."

"An' we're plain dust, Sally."

"When I marry," Alan said, "whichever dust she is, she'll have to promise to come to the Harris reunion with me—*and like it.*"

"When *you* marry, Alan, all the Harrises will be reunioning in heaven!" teased Sally.

"It might be sooner than you think, Sally—"

Martha, straining to hear more, was disappointed that Chester let the screen door bang, his frown bordering on a scowl. Alan and Sally's eyes asked for an explanation. "Candice insists that I come home today."

"Today?" blurted Nellie. "Oh, Chester, not today! We have these children who need attending to—I can't care for them by myself—"

"I told Candice so. I explained that it would be next week before I could possibly get away. And I'm afraid she is quite angry with me for putting my work before her plans."

"But is it so . . . important?" Alan chose his words gingerly.

"Material things." He shook his head. "There's a prime piece of property just come up for sale in the heart of the city. She wants me to negotiate for it for a hospital.

148

She's afraid it will sell before I get home."

"A hospital? Your own hospital?"

"I think that's what Candice—and her mother—have in mind. Can you imagine a *Harris* hospital?"

"If you could give me instructions, Chester," Nellie offered, "I can try to take care of your patients here as best I can so that you can go on. I wouldn't want you to miss an oportunity to—"

"No. My work isn't complete until I have this baby out of the woods, and I refuse to leave an unfinished task. If the baby should die, I would feel responsible if I had not done everything in my power to save him—and I would be responsible as a doctor. After this, I have one more . . . project. Then Alan can run me into the Springs to catch the train. And if the property is gone . . . well, so be it." His resolute look gave no room for compromise.

"Now, Alan, if you could run down to the river and tell the Taylors that I need these children for a bit longer. Another day should put us in the homestretch. If they'd like to bring the buggy up closer, Mama'll see that they have plenty of food."

Alan left, thoughts churning in his mind. He knew that the phone call had torn Chester apart. Chester had his heart set on being a country doctor; he loved best what he was doing at this moment. But his wife was determined that he should have a famous hospital profession, complete with his own laboratory in the center of the busy city.

Chester had excused himself from church the Sunday past, saying he had some reading to do on a new surgical procedure. Alan suspected he didn't wish to face his wife's scorn when she learned that he had attended the country church with its nonseminarian preacher.

Should one sacrifice his ideals—his very soul—for a wife? Should any woman ask so much of a man? Was Chester truly happy, or were all these concessions his price for a peaceful coexistence with the proud woman? Did anyone really know how expensive Chester's domestic tranquility had become?

So deep and so troubled were Alan's thoughts that he arrived at the river scarcely remembering why he had come. His heart beat a little faster. Would she be here?

No, he'd been sent with a message to the Taylors about their grandchildren, he remembered with a suddenness that blotted out all other thoughts.

He looked about, expecting to see Oscar and Rufus playing in the water, waiting to hear their yells as they splashed each other. The liquid games kept them occupied and, therefore, oblivious to more serious matters.

But everything was quiet this morning. The frogs and the birds had the airwaves to themselves.

The buggy had been moved; he expected to find it tucked away in the shinnery somewhere, its occupants resting late. It should be easy to find if he followed the tracks away through the river banks' soft grasses. Probably they wanted a bit more privacy.

But he followed the newly-made tracks all the way to the road—and they kept going. Mr. Taylor had likely gone into town for supplies, Alan decided. The boys or Eva Taylor might be wandering about picking early blackberries. Or napping on a pallet. He called, but the only response he got was the echo of his own voice.

Alan wove his way back to the campsite to wait for Mr. Taylor's return. However, he noticed that Mr. Taylor had carefully covered the fire pit with dirt as a prevention against a grass fire. The area was clean and barren, showing no sign of their planned reestablishment.

Alan was puzzled. Surely they hadn't left without Susan and the baby. *Or had they?*

CHAPTER NINETEEN

The Note

Alan made another circle.

When he started back toward the footpath, trying to put some order to the turn of events, he saw the tattered note sheet anchored between two large rocks.

Had I not been so preoccupied with Chester's dilemma, he told himself, *I would have noticed these stones on the way to the river.* They were right beside the path.

The note, scrawled in uneven letters by Eva Taylor, explained that she had "weighed her soul" and decided what God wanted her to do. She wished to "give" the sick children to Nellie Harris. Convinced that she "wouldn't be in this here world much longer" and was too "used up and ailing" to provide them proper care, she was sure that Nellie would provide them "mother love." "Nellie told me she wanted some children," the message said. "She's got some now, and I hope they bring her happiness." There was a postscript, scribbled in a larger, bolder print that Alan supposed was Mr. Taylor's. It said: "Sorry we ain't got no money to leave for their care."

Alan read the note twice. The preposterousness of it set his mind to spinning like a dust devil. He wrestled with the revelation of Eva Taylor's plan. The grandparents had deliberately abandoned the unhealthy children but took the strapping boys with them. Alan had showed kindness to the unfortunate strangers, and now they had dumped their unwanted burden on Nellie. Anger and pity teamed together to pull Alan's thoughts along.

What if his sister-in-law did not wish to rear someone else's children? She and William would want their own.

What should he do? Where did Mr. Taylor say they were headed? To Milton? No. Milburn? No, that wasn't it, either. *Milford.* That was the place. They had come from the west, so would they head north, south, or east when they reached the main road?

Mr. Taylor said they bought chicken feed in this town. That might provide a clue as to their whereabouts; the personnel at the feed store might be able to tell him how to locate the deserters. Perhaps he and William could overtake them and bring them back to face up to their responsibility. Hank had a couple of fast steeds.

What would it be like, though, to be a small child brought up by someone who didn't want the bother of you? Surely these sick children deserved better. And then, maybe the Taylors felt they were acting in the best interest of the children. Any inexperienced eye could see that Mrs. Taylor was quite ill. The children *would* be better off with William—if his brother wanted them.

How long had the Taylors been gone? Alan suspected they left under the cover of darkness and, if so, could have an advantageous jump on anyone who tried to overtake them. Well, he'd have to go tell Chester and his mother and—Nellie.

He started for the house—running in a daze of unreality—and failed to see Molly coming down an intersecting trail. Her mouth fell open in surprise as she watched Alan's sprinting exit. She hesitated as if trying to decide whether to follow him or not. Then she turned and headed back toward the old corduroy bridge toward her grandmother's house.

"Nellie!" Alan called as he entered Sally's cottage.

"I sent her over to Mama's to get a few winks of sleep, Alan. She was up all night again with the sick baby. She won't sleep long, though." Sally gave her head a nod toward Martha's house.

"The baby is better?"

"I think so. Chester gives him a fighting chance now. His temperature has lowered. Do you need Nellie for something?"

"Yes, but I won't wake her up. Where's William?"

"He has gone to Hank's to fetch Michael so Chester can have a look at his ankle. I declare, Alan, we have a regular hospital going here!" She laughed. "A *Harris* hospital. And Chester is loving every minute of it!"

"I—hope so. I need to talk with him, too."

Sally threw her hand toward the south bedroom. "He's in Room One, making his morning rounds. Nurse Sally is getting Room Two ready for another emergency case due in promptly. Room Three is the examining room. If you're going to be here a few minutes, I need to step over to Mama's and get some clean rags. We're working short-handed."

"I'll be around," Alan grinned at his sister, who was not only the youngest but also the prettiest of the Harris girls. "Dr. Chester has a lovely nurse. I hope she is as

155

efficient as she is beautiful. If it should fall my lot to become hospitalized, I'll put in for her as my special." He disappeared into the bedroom, ignoring the face she made at him.

Chester looked up, hollow eyed but cheerful. His hair, with a precocious will of its own, fell over his forehead in disarray. "This tyke may make it, brother. Why, he may live to be as old as Granny Myrt—and overtop you and me for height. Look at these long fingers!"

"We pray he won't hit as many sour notes on the organ."

"Are the Taylors coming up to see him this morning?"

"The Taylors are gone."

"That's all right. I need to keep this baby a while longer anyhow. They'll be surprised by his progress when they get back. Why, Alan, the little mite of a fellow tried to smile at me this morning when I put the stethoscope on his tummy!"

"But Chester, you don't understand. The Taylors are *gone.*"

"Let them stay gone a week for all I care. That will give me more time with these patients of mine. I want to examine the little girl, too—"

"They won't be back in a week."

"Oh, Nellie won't mind seeing after them a bit longer if I have to leave. She's in her element. Happy as an old setting hen. She surprises me! She's superb with babies."

"Chester, the Taylors have—"

Just then, Nellie, looking short of sleep but ready to take up where she had left off, came through the doorway. "How's the young gentleman?" she asked Chester.

"He may make it, Nellie."

Tears badgered Nellie's cobalt eyes. "I've prayed so hard that he would live!"

"Nellie, I need to warn you about getting too attached to this baby—too bonded. It—it won't be good for you. The Taylors have gone, but they'll be back to get these children—"

The note that Alan pulled from his pocket crackled. Somehow, he had to make Chester understand what he had been trying to say. "Chester, I never did get to finish my story. I'm glad Nellie is here to hear it because it concerns her and William—"

"If the story is very long, let me get the baby into my arms and get to the rocking chair." Nellie picked up the infant, who tried to gurgle at her. "I want to pack as much love as I can into this flash-in-the-pan motherhood. Don't worry about me, Chester. I know this is just for a few hours, but it may be the last chance I have in a lifetime to be a mother—"

"Nellie, Chester sent me to tell the Taylors that he needed the children for a few more days and that they were welcome to move closer in for the duration. They had already moved but not closer in, I'm afraid. They're gone—lock, stock, and barrel. They must have left sometime during the night."

The Taylor's purpose and intent was as far removed from Nellie's imagination as it had been from Chester's. "They had business, doubtless. They knew we'd care for these children until their return. Oh, joy! A few more days with this precious baby!" She bent to kiss the petite head.

Alan held up the dirty paper. "According to the message they left between two rocks, they're gone for good and the children are all yours, Nellie. Evidently, we have two new family members, ready or not. That's what I call *instant children!*"

The enormity of Alan's statement settled on Nellie by degrees. "You mean . . . you mean . . ."

"Yes, I mean," laughed Alan.

Chester grinned a slow grin. "What will you name your new son, Nellie?"

"Don't tease, Chester. I'm afraid to hope. They might change their minds and come back for—for my children—or the baby might—might die yet." Her emotions crumbled.

"And here I was worried that you might not want someone else's children!" Alan said.

"Alan! I've been praying five years for this day!"

"Then why do you fear that God will snatch your answer away, Nellie?" He smiled at the impact of his own words. "Here's the note. Hold it in your hands. Read it for yourself. I was half afraid William and I would have to track the Taylors down and refuse their kind offer."

"Never, Alan."

"But you haven't talked to William yet."

"Yes, I have! He gave his approval in the middle of the night last night. He prayed a beautiful prayer for this baby's recovery then said to me: 'Don't you wish he could be our own?' So there!" She combined a laugh and a cry. "And," she looked sheepish, "we've already named him William Gibson Harris. We'll call him Billy."

Chester chuckled but quickly sobered. He gave Nellie a steady look. "But I hope, Nellie, that you can manage the older one, too. She will need special attention."

"Oh, I love her dearly, Chester!"

"But you must face the fact that she may never talk.

I have not heard her utter a sound. She may not have the capacity to speak; she may have no voice box."

"I'll love her no less whether she can talk or whether she can't talk."

"I like that kind of spunk." Chester rubbed his chin. "I sort of made a deal with God this morning. If He'll let me fix up these children—take them to normal health— I'll go back to church."

No one said a word, and suddenly Chester slapped one fist into the palm of his other hand. "No!"

Astonished at his outburst, Alan and Nellie waited, speechless and troubled.

"Who am I to try to bargain with God? I am a mere mortal! God doesn't have to come to my terms. What am I thinking? I should make my peace with Him whether He helps me or whether He doesn't. And I will. From now on, no one will come between me and my God! Not even my wife. A soul is not to be trifled with. Candice won't answer for me at judgment. I will have to answer for myself. I'm coming *home*, Alan. . . ."

Alan smiled. "You don't know how glad it makes me to hear those words. God will stand by you, and on those terms, He'll probably hear your prayers for these children."

Back at the house, Martha could keep her worries to herself no longer. While Sally stripped old cup towels into rags, Martha confided to her, "I guess Alan's keepin' a secret from usns, Sally-girl. I heared his talkin' to that Helen-girl on th' horn 'bout them getting' married when he gets back t' Austin. My, but a mother has lots o' worries."

"Seems you haven't but one single worry, Mama. And

that's your single Alan. The one I'm worried about right now is Nellie. She's wrapped her heartstrings around those sick children, and when they are gone, they will take her heart right along with them.''

CHAPTER TWENTY

Fading Hopes

"What did you learn about these children? About their family?" Sally asked her mother.

"Scanty little," Martha answered. "Even th' gra'ma don't know much. Susan has th' Taylor name. Th' two boys, Rufus an' Oscar, was first named after their gran'pas on their mother's side o' th' fam'ly an' they're last-named Adams. Th' baby ain't named at all, first ner last. Ifn it lives, I guess it'll be Taylor-named."

"And if it doesn't . . . make it, the marker will say 'unnamed Taylor Boy'?"

"Won't be no marker lessn we put him in our own plot—which is what I plan to do. He's one of God's little uns an' deserves a unlonely place in God's earth. Nellie is so heart-hung to it, she may want to mark it Harris-fer-a-day so's she'll have a baby to get up with on resurrectin' morn."

"You don't suppose, do you, Mama, that those boys could have been akin to *Eli* Adams?"

"Well, now, I hadn't give it no thought." She

appeared to be considering Sally's question. "But if favor means anything, they shore could be kin alrighty."

"You're saying they looked like Eli?"

"I didn't stare 'um straight in th' face, but yes'm, they did look like Eli Adams."

The door clapper interrupted the talk.

"Company, Sally. Ifn it was one of ourn, they'd walk right in without knockin'. Go see who calls on us."

Molly's perfume traveled ahead of her like an escort. She followed close behind. "I just stopped in to see if everything is all right with you, Mrs. Harris—" she began.

"Jest peachy, Molly. With all my children t' home, I couldn't ask fer nothin' better, thank you."

"Oh, good. That is . . . I was down at the riv—, I mean, I was passing along the road a short while ago and saw Alan running quite hurriedly toward the house. I was afraid that he may have gotten word that you were ill or—"

"Like as not he'd been hisself a-fishin' or checkin' his trot lines. Prob'ly t' little boy jest riz up in him an' made him want to run. When he gets back to th' city, he can't run like that."

Molly's brows crawled up under her low-hanging bangs. "Fishing?" Amusement hid poorly behind the question.

"Alan likes to fish," explained Sally. "He'd likely had Michael with him if Michael wasn't laid up with a bad foot. I've never seen any two people like to fish better than those."

Still bemused, Molly said, "I think Michael might not be invited this year."

"I don't see why not." Martha's dislike for Molly bled

162

through. "Michael is his *nephew*."

Molly looked from Sally to Martha and back again, sensing an unspoken unity. Sally would probably join allegiance with her mother against her and Alan if tit came to tat. Sally had a religious streak now that had been missing in their teenage years when they would cover for each other. This concerned Molly. She decided she needed to sew up some raveled edges to take the guesswork out of her uncertain marital status. And now was the time to do it.

"And, too, I came to let you know, Sally, that I got the official notice of Eli's death. He was killed several months ago. He fell from a pole. It is most unfortunate for me, and I haven't been able to bring myself to talk about it."

"How is it that you are just now getting the word, Molly?"

Molly didn't flinch. "We had moved, and Eli failed to give the company our new location—"

"It seems you would have been in contact with them for his check, anyhow."

Sally was a perceptive one, all right. Too perceptive.

"I think I *felt* it, Sally. Remember what I whispered to you in the wagon? I *sensed* that Eli was gone, and I went into denial. Isn't that what they call it when you don't want to believe that something precious has been taken from your life? The fact is I've been running all this time, *pretending* that Eli is not really dead. I've been running from myself. That's why I came here."

"They didn't even try to call your grandmother when—when Eli was killed?"

"They did call, but she is so forgetful she can't even

remember getting the call."

"I'm sorry, Molly." Martha's words, almost mumbled, were contrite and full of genuine sympathy. "I been through it. I know how a widow feels. An' you so young. At least I got t' keep my Henry through ten children an' a heap o' years o' memory an' happiness."

Molly was dry-eyed. "It's like Granny Myrt says, Mrs. Harris, there's life beyond death. When one is young like I am, one bounces back faster. My life has to go on even though Eli's has ended. And I'm ready to go on with it now. That's what Eli would wish me to do. That's what he told me to do if anything ever happened to him."

"But never will it be th' same." Martha shook her head.

"Molly," Sally threw in the question off-handed, "was Eli ever married before you met him?"

"Before? Before *me*, you mean?"

"Yes."

"Oh, no. I was his only woman. I'm the only one he ever loved enough to marry."

"Did he ever mention a woman named Mattie?"

Molly's eyes betrayed her. "No," she lied. Then, not knowing what knowledge Sally might have obtained, she added, "Once he got a letter forwarded by the telephone company from a Mattie Adams, but he said he had never heard of the person and the company had made a mistake."

"What did the letter say?"

What did Sally know? "She just mentioned two little boys. It was all quite ridiculous. . . ."

"Were their names Rufus and Oscar?"

Molly blanched. "Look, if you're trying to work up

a case against my Eli, you can forget it. He was always honest as Abe with me, and he would have had no call to deceive me about a previous family. He's dead now, anyhow, and if he had children, the company would have found them and notified *them* of his departure."

"When I worked for the telephone company," Sally went on with maddening aplomb, "I met a woman in a restaurant who knew Mattie Adams personally." Sally dropped a well-planned pause that thundered louder than words. "I should think if Eli had two boys, they might benefit from the company's generous insurance plan for surviving dependents. They take good care of orphaned children."

"Drop it, Sally!" Molly's tone turned cruel now. "For crying aloud, can't you let the poor man rest in peace? There was a big mixup, okay? There's evidently another Eli Adams somewhere in the world . . ." Her face was red and angry.

"Don't ruffle 'er, Sally, with her a-fresh grievin'," Martha said.

That's when Alan came in the back door. He stopped, puzzled. "Is there a problem, Molly?" he asked. The solicitude unnerved Martha.

"No," she gave him a tight, cool smile. "I just—well, never mind. I came by to see if something was . . . was wrong with *you*."

"With *me*."

"You left the river awfully fast today. I was coming to—"

Alan cut her off with a jest. "I had a message that was itching to be scratched at Sally's place. Who were the runners in the Bible: the one running with good news and the other with bad? I had news that I couldn't decide which was which."

"News?" Martha patted the white collar on her blue dress. It was a matter of habit.

"Yes, Mama. It looks as though you are going to have two new grandchildren on the same day!"

The words sank in. "Sarah? Amy? Pauline? Candice? Lucy? Dessie?" She stopped. "You, Sally?"

Sally's hands flew to her waistline. "Not me, Mama!"

Alan laughed. "Guess again."

"That's all."

"Nellie!"

"Now I know you're joshin', Alan. An' twins at that!"

"The Taylors left sometime during the night. They left a note giving both of the children that are here to Nellie."

"They *what*?" Sally jumped up and grabbed Alan's arm. "What are you talking about, Alan?"

"Mrs. Taylor didn't feel able to rear the sickly ones, so they gave them to Nellie and went on their way during the night or early this morning."

"What a lovely surprise for Nellie!" Molly filled the shocked silence.

"I wasn't certain whether or not Nellie would want them, but I needn't have worried!"

"I shouldn't wonder that she would." Molly carried the conversational ball with Alan. "If I had a home to offer, I would be happy to take in the poor orphans. What a philanthropic thing to do!"

"Nellie said they were an answer to her prayers."

"Well, glory be!" shouted Martha, at last recovering her voice. "Like Effie used t' say, God sure answers prayers *pretty*. They couldn't'a found two sweeter ones nowhere. I jest knew th' good Lord had some younguns somewhere tagged fer William an' Nellie. What did William say when he learnt about it, Alan?''

"William doesn't know about it yet."

"Lawsy me! A doubled-up family an' him not even knowin' he's a paw! But he'll be proud as Nellie or my name ain't Marthy Harris. I bound ye he'll pop off some buttons an' strut.''

"They named the new one William Gibson. I think they plan to call him Billy.''

"*They?* I thought you said William didn't know.''

"They named him in the middle of the night. Last night. Just sort of wishing and funning.''

"He's . . . he's gonna live, then?''

"Chester says most probably he will. And all because Nellie wouldn't let him die.''

"Why, that's reason for a party, Alan!''

"Yes, let's have a party." Molly's eyes crinkled at the edges. "Alan, you do make a handsome uncle!''

"They're such beautiful children they'd make any uncle glow in the dark, Molly. Have you seen them?''

"No, but I shall be happy to." Molly took this as her personal invitation to the welcoming party. "I hope that I shall have such a lovely niece and nephew to dote upon someday.''

"Oh, you will!" Caught up in the contagion of his sister-in-law's rapture, Alan smiled a most engaging smile.

Molly took the smile and parked it at the front steps of her own ego.

When the girls had gone, Martha sat down at the

kitchen table, her soul battered in a cyclone of swirling emotions. She put her head on her arms and let her single worry consume her.

Amy found her there. "You are tired from so many to care for," she said. "We should have been carrying more of the load. What may I do, Mama Harris?"

"No, Amy, it's not physical tired. It's spirit tired. I had so looked forward t' all o' you being' here an' I had this teeny notion that Alan might . . . might find hisself a helpmeet—"

"Who would Alan find here in Brazos Point or in The Springs?"

"I'd laid a hope on th' new schoolteacher. We did ever'thing we could to give 'um matchin'-up chances: th' party at Sarah's, church, dinner . . . an' nothin' worked. You was a schoolteacher an' you made sech a right wife fer Joseph. . . ."

"Miss Young is already spoken for, Mama Harris."

"She—she *what?*"

"She told me when I went to school the other day that she will marry someone whom her father chose for her before he died. I think she feels rather duty bound to carry out his wishes."

"That wouldn't seem right, would it, fer her father t' leave her named to some man, with him gone on an' all?"

"It's as if . . . as if she would feel guilty if she didn't fulfill his wishes. She loved her father very much."

"I never heared nobody talkin' of her plans."

"Elise is a quiet, lovely young lady. Probably nobody bothered to ask her. She hasn't been here long enough to establish close friendships."

"I knowed she was always radiant an' happy—an' always eager fer th' mail." Martha squared her wilting shoulders. "Well, someone's gettin' a good un. I'm happy fer 'um. Jest wisht it could'a been mine." The lump in her throat felt as big as a double-yolked egg.

"God has just the right wife picked out for Alan, Mama Harris. And we can't always help Him with His projects. Remember Sarah in the Bible? She got in God's way trying to help Him get her a son. She forgot that He is capable of carrying out His promises all by Himself. It may not seem like it, but everything will turn out well for Alan. Just you wait and see!"

CHAPTER TWENTY ONE

The Search

Eli Adams sat on a barstool in the Starboard Lounge, trying to focus his blurry vision on the room-length mirror that covered the entire back wall. His head felt too large for his body and too heavy. Having lost most of his money gambling in a game called forty-two, he considered what to do next.

He could hear the tinkling of glasses and the slapping of cards against a table, but the sounds seemed to crawl away. Somewhere someone plucked away at a banjo with three monotonous chords. It was getting on his nerves.

He ordered a cup of coffee, and while the bartender—a sloshy man with little dumplings under his eyes—went for it, Eli looked into the mirror and tried to imagine a woman sitting beside him. With effort he tried to put a face on her.

He was still quite handsome, he noted with egocentric pride, his inkberry eyes and black curly hair being the most redeeming of his features.

He had just returned from a trip to Seminole in search

of Mattie, one of the wives on his deserted spouse list.

He had met Mattie, a single girl with a baby daughter who never learned to talk, in Waco. With matched spirits, they ran the gamut of taverns. When he realized he couldn't shake her, he married her. There had been a baby born, a boy; when he learned that a second was on the way, he took her to Seminole, a forsaken place on the border of West Texas and New Mexico and left her there in a ratty one-roomed shack. He found diversion elsewhere and did not return for her.

What sentimentality made him go back to look for her after seven errant years he could not explain even to himself.

When he reached the windblown prairie town, he found that Mattie had died. Her parents, Earl and Eva Taylor, had come for the children. He told himself he was glad. His interest was not in the boys but only in what more he could drain from Mattie, financially or otherwise.

Eli wandered about town, picking up fragments of talk, some of which, he supposed, were meant to incriminate him. Mattie had remarried, a town gossip said, but her husband had "slipped the noose" before Mattie gave birth to her fourth child, a feeble baby boy. After her husband abandoned her, Mattie got "religion."

"She was a reg'lar preacher woman after she joined up with that Holy Roller bunch," the informant told Eli. "Dressed tow-sack plain, all covered up neck to ankles, took off her paint, bunned her hair, an' stopped her honky-tonking."

Eli couldn't imagine Mattie in such a lifestyle. It boggled his mind. Mattie . . . at *church*?

"I'll have to admit, she was peaceful, always smilin'

and downright pretty," the gossip said. "Said she had wasted her whole life on sin and the devil, but she would never live for Satan again. It made this whole town sit up and notice."

After he heard that report, Eli was glad he hadn't found her. In such a holy condition, she certainly would not have served his purposes. He wanted nothing to do with God.

He left Seminole and marked Mattie off his list. Most of his other lady friends had gone on to other phases of life, and sitting here at the bar, he suffered a surge of loneliness. He felt left out. Life . . . youth . . . something was slipping away.

Then a vision of Molly Rushing came into his besotted head. Ah, dear Molly! Of all his exes, she was probably the most beautiful . . . and the most untamable. Dolly Molly, he'd called her. Insubordination flowed in her veins like the sodas she dispensed at the drugstores. But she was free-spirited—and desirable! *Now that one,* he told himself, *I didn't keep long enough to get a leash around her pretty neck!*

And didn't she say she was in line for some sort of inheritance? The old grandmother must be nearly a hundred years old, and then there would be land and some money to boot. Why had he let all this slip through his fingers?

He could almost see Molly sitting there now, pulling the wineglass to her red, red lips, her dark hair falling almost into her big, violet eyes. What a picture!

"I'll go find her," he said aloud, "and get her back."

"What did you say, sir?" the barkeeper asked.

"Did I say something?" Eli, faintly surprised, got up

and left immediately on unsteady legs. He couldn't afford to be caged up in a paddy wagon now. He had to find Molly.

He'd left her in Austin, so that's where he would start his search. The drugstores would be his best source of information, he reasoned, so he started from one to the other, hoping he could walk off some of the effects of the alcohol.

In a cloistered cafe near the capitol building, he met two girls whom he figured ranged in the vicinity of Molly's age. He interrupted their whispers and giggles long enough to ask if they knew Molly. They said yes, they had seen a young lady named Molly Rushing with crowblack hair, but no, they didn't know where she lived, and no, it hadn't been this week. It had been about two weeks ago.

At least she's still in Austin, Eli satisfied himself.

At one soda fountain, a fish-eyed boy knew a lot about Molly and directed Eli to her living quarters. He gave Eli a sly wink. "She may have moved on to another job," he said. "I haven't seen her around for several days."

In a hungry hurry, Eli followed the directions to a flat not far removed from the city's red-light district. He squinted at the number he had written down against the one on the door and decided he was at the right address.

When he knocked, a muffled voice invited him to "come on in," and he expected to find Molly half asleep or burrowing from under a bout of drunkenness.

But the shrunken girl in the disheveled daybed bore no resemblance to Molly. Unprotected by makeup, her face was chalky and lifeless. Mousy brown springs of hair escaped from a dirty scarf, and her arms were spindly without the shape of a woman in them anywhere. The

174

sight repulsed and vexed Eli. He was accustomed to much more streamlined women.

"Pardon me." He started to back up toward the door. "I have the wrong address."

"For whom are you looking?" The woman's words were flat and slow. "I'm Adema."

"A demon?" Eli jumped. "I—I—" His hands shook.

"Mister, I'm not *that* bad." She coughed, a rasping sound that made something rattle around inside her chest.

"Would you happen to know where I might find Miss Molly Rushing? Or Molly Adams?"

"Yep. She lives here with me. There's her bunk." She turned her head toward the bed across the cluttered room. "She's not here right now, but if you're a customer of hers, I would be glad to—"

"She's my *wife!*" Eli blurted. "And I need to find her soon! Now tell me where she is!"

"She didn't tell me she was married," Adema said, undaunted by Eli's outburst. "Why, I can't imagine why she would ever let a gorgeous hunk like you get away and live this kind of rat's life. She must be crazy. Now, if *I* had a husband like you—hon, just give me a chance and see how fast I could light a shuck out of here."

"Well, I'm not interested in anybody but my Dolly Molly. And if you don't get busy and tell me where my wife is, it'll be all the demons to pay!"

"Sir, she went to see her grandmother. I've forgotten the name of the place. Some country town. . . ."

"I know where her grandmother lives. It's Brazos Point."

"That's the place. Seems she told the boss that the old lady was sick or dying and she needed to check on the will or something. I had expected she'd be back by now. She's been gone past her limit of time, but she can always get by the boss somehow. He's holding her position open for her at the fountain yet. She brings him more customers than any of the other waitresses or all of them put together. But who knows, maybe she got the money and skipped. That's what I'd do if I had the chance." Adema went into another spasm of coughing. "I hope she comes back before long, though, because the rent is due on this place next week, and I can't pay it all by myself. It was our agreement that she'd do half."

"Don't expect Molly back at all, Demon," Eli said. "I have my plans to find her and take her back into my loving arms. Oh, she'll try to elude me, all right, but I'll convince her that we can have fun spending that inherited money together. My charms work again and again."

He strode out, gave the door a wicked slam, and headed for the train station.

CHAPTER TWENTY TWO

The Diagnosis

"Nellie, you take t' motherin' like a moonshiner t' mash," Martha quipped. Indeed, Nellie was intoxicated with her newly acquired motherhood.

"Yes, I'm afraid I'm already addicted," Nellie agreed. "And William is as fussy over them as I am. This is one reunion we'll never forget."

"Since your baby is on the mend, Nellie, I want to concentrate on Susan in the short time before I have to leave." Chester straightened his back from bending over Billy. "If you'll round her up and bring her in, we'll see what we can learn."

However, when the time came for the examination, Susan was nowhere to be found.

"She's off follerin' th' wee kitten somewhere," predicted Martha. "I never seen a child so lovin' of animals. She thinks she has t' protect th' cats while Matilda is at school."

Nellie began her search for the girl. She looked in the front yard and back then headed for the outbuildings. As

she approached the barn, she heard a strange sound. At first she thought it was a bird calling. "Keee . . . keee
. . . ."

The call came closer, and as Nellie rounded the corner of the barn, she met Susan. "Keee?" Susan said and shrugged her shoulders in an exasperated hunch.

The surprise of the sound obscured all other astonishments. When Nellie realized that Susan had actually uttered it, she scooped the child into her arms and began to sob joyfully.

Susan, perhaps thinking that her beloved kitten had come to some infamous end, began to cry, too.

"My precious daughter!" cried Nellie. "You did it! You made a *sound!*"

Susan seemed thoroughly puzzled, still looking this way and that for the straying cat.

"Call again," encouraged the overjoyed mother. "Maybe we'll find that naughty runaway!"

"Keee . . . keee . . . keee. . . ."

Nellie was sure she had never heard a more beautiful sound.

"Keee!" Susan pointed to the yawning feline, who stretched one back leg and then the other as she crawled from beneath a rotted board and made her way toward them. The cat stopped to clean her face with delicate sweeps of her paw then began chasing her tail. Susan snatched her up. "Mmmm. Keee." She buried her face in the ball of fur.

Nellie couldn't get back to Chester fast enough. "Chester!" she crowed. "Susan made a sound!"

"Are you sure, Nellie? We don't want to base our hopes on wishful thinking."

"I'm positive, Chester. She called the kitten."

"What did she say?"

"She said, 'Keee . . . keee . . . .' "

Chester laughed. "That's mighty good news, Nellie, even if she just made a phonetic sound. Let's get her in here and have a look at her."

Susan came at Nellie's beck, kitten and all. "If the kitten gives her any comfort, let her hang on to it," Chester advised. "The child has been through enough trauma for a lifetime already, Nellie."

Chester began his examination by asking simple questions. He asked Susan to tell him how old she was by holding up her fingers. She sat the cat down gently and held up eight fingers.

"Now, Susan, Uncle Chester won't hurt you. Nobody here will hurt you. I just want to see what we can do to help you learn to talk better. Do you understand?"

She nodded.

"Your mother tells me that you did a great job of calling your kitty." He stopped and smiled. Susan returned the smile, a trusting look in her eyes. "You're a very pretty girl, and Uncle Chester is glad you've come to live with William and Nellie. William is my big brother." Her eyes showed that she grasped everything he said. *Nothing wrong with her comprehension,* he noted mentally.

"Now I'll take the cat over here to the other side of the room, and you call her to you." He removed the cat to the opposite wall.

"Keee . . . keee . . ." called Susan, and the bit of fur scampered toward her. Nellie flashed Chester a triumphant I-told-you-so look.

"*Very* good!" encouraged the doctor. "Can you make other noises, Susan?"

179

"Um-hum." She didn't open her mouth.

"What would you call her?" Chester pointed to Nellie.

"Maaa."

Nellie's tearful hug interrupted Chester's interview.

"What is this?" Chester pointed to a chair. Susan shook her head and wouldn't try to make a sound.

"You can't say it?"

"Naaa." Susan looked frustrated.

"That's all right, honey. We don't expect you to say anything you can't."

The child's face showed relief. Nellie gave her brother-in-law an appreciative smile. *He is so good with children,* she thought. *He should be a children's doctor.*

"And if you got scared in the middle of the night, and you needed Daddy William, how would you call him?"

"PAAA!" She screamed it.

Nothing wrong with her volume either. Chester added to his unwritten notes.

Nellie cried again.

"Maaa?" Susan asked, concerned.

"She's crying because she's happy. Some new mothers act that way. It's the mystery of motherhood. You'll just have to accept her as she is, Susan." This brought a tearful laugh from Nellie.

Susan nodded with a crooked smile of her own.

"Now Uncle Chester will have to look down your throat. I'll put this little stick on your tongue, but it won't hurt. Open up your mouth. That's right."

When Chester had looked all about Susan's mouth, he began to chuckle. The chuckle grew into a full-throated laugh. "Nellie! Nellie! You're not going to believe this!"

"What, Chester? And why are you laughing?" Chester

180

realized then that Nellie's nerves were as taut as a bowstring.

"Do you remember the man in the Bible—I believe it's in the Book of Mark—that our Lord healed—?"

"He healed so many, Chester!"

"The one who had the speech impediment."

"I can't recall that one in particular. What has that to do with Susan's healing?"

"Jesus loosed the *string of his tongue* so that he could speak clearly. There's nothing wrong with this child except that I need to clip the string underneath her tongue. It's holding the tongue down completely. That keeps her from talking."

"Chester! Are you saying that she will be able to talk?"

"Perfectly, unless I've missed my diagnosis."

"Will there be a . . . a lot of pain?"

"We'll see that there isn't. It will heal amazingly fast, Nellie. And nicely. Children are resilient. And this one is in astonishingly good health."

"And she's brave."

"Susan," Chester explained, "you will be able to talk as well as Matilda when your uncle gets you all fixed up. But we'll have to put you to sleep for a few minutes and work on the bottom of your tongue. Is that all right?"

Susan weighed the options. Her eyes clouded and cleared, clouded and cleared again. Slowly she nodded her head yes.

"I'll get the surgical tray ready, Nellie, while you find the spirits of nitre in my bag there."

He whistled a tune.

How lucky we are to have a doctor in our family, Nellie thought.

CHAPTER TWENTY THREE

The Shower

Word of William's "double-blessing family" got out with partyline speed, and an immediate shower was planned for the new parents.

Treadle machines went into a clatter of action as dresses and gowns took shape from feed sacks and outgrown frocks. A touch of ribbon here and a bit of lace there turned the creations into catalogue-perfect outfits for Susan and blankets and nightshirts for Billy.

Neighbors brought cake and cookies, and men and boys cranked away at the growling ice cream freezers. Martha declared the occasion "better'n a barn raisin'."

Molly, the first to arrive, made excuses for her grandmother's absence, but Martha suspected the self-bitten granddaughter left Myrt behind so she would not be constricted to the older woman's schedule. Myrt's strength always played out before Molly's flirtation did.

Martha bade the girl make herself at home and left her looking at the gallery of family portraits on the parlor wall.

When Sally came in, Molly called her over to the display. "This must be Chester's wife; I don't believe I've met her."

"Yes, that's Candice," Sally nodded.

"Very sophisticated looking. I'm sure I would like her. And Arthur has a beautiful wife, too."

"We think so. Lucy was the mayor's daughter from the Gap, but she fits right in with the family."

"This is a fine picture of Alan, but it seems so . . . so out of place!" She cut her eyes toward Sally.

"I don't know why you should say that, Molly."

"All the others are couples or families. Alan is all alone."

Sally laughed. "We call him Mama's 'single worry.' She's afraid he'll be a bachelor. He's almost thirty."

"Oh, there's no chance of bachelorhood for Alan!" cooed Molly. "Now that Eli is gone, I'd be glad to be a part of his life in Austin. Isn't it a coincidence, Sally, that fate has put us in the same town?"

Before Sally could answer, Martha ushered in Elise Young, Pastor and Mrs. Stevens, and Matthew's family. Sally noted that Molly only gave Elise an indifferent nod. But Elise didn't seem to feel slighted. She joined Molly for a look at the wall collage.

"The Harrises have a lovely family, don't they?"

"Delightful! I've known them all my life. I was just telling Sally that I wouldn't mind taking Alan off their hands. You know, we live and work in the same town, and it would be awfully convenient for both of us if we could blend our lives."

"I should think that marriage would be more sacred than a thing of convenience." Elise said it sweetly with

184

no condemnation. "At least, mine will be."

"Oh, are you planning marriage, Miss Young? I didn't know—"

"Yes, if God wills."

"If God wills? I don't see that He has anything to do with it. You meet somebody, you fall in love, you have a ceremony—it's all quite a human development, something God leaves up to us."

"I beg to disagree without being disagreeable, Miss Rushing. You see, I belong to God, and He has a right to say who I should marry and who I shouldn't. I wouldn't like to make so momentous a decision by myself."

"Why, I've never heard anything quite so . . . so . . . " Molly searched for a word, ". . . unusual. Suppose you loved someone, and God said—however He speaks—that you shouldn't marry that someone?"

"Then I'm sure I wouldn't."

"Even if you wished very much to marry that individual?"

"I would have to have God's approval. Otherwise my life would be outside the perimeter of His blessings."

"Does God tell you everything to do?"

"I should like for Him to, yes."

"I mean, your job and all?"

"I pray about everything. And I certainly feel that He sent me to Brazos Point. My life has been enriched. I've learned to know the Harrises, the Stevenses, the Gibsons, your grandmother," she smiled, "and now I've met you."

Others were coming, and Alan entered the room, giving Nellie a quick thumbs-up signal. Molly excused herself from Elise and rushed to his side.

"This is the welcoming party we planned for those dear children." She meant for her voice to reach everyone in the room. "Remember that day? The day you told your mother the good news of her new grandchildren?"

Alan tilted his head. "I'm glad you could come, Molly. I wish Granny Myrt could have come along, too. It just doesn't seem complete without her."

"She would have fallen asleep before the party got started! She goes down with the sun." Molly winked. "And when you have time, Alan, I need to talk with you about our return trip to Austin so that I can make my reservations ahead of time—"

Martha stopped what she was doing to listen.

"I'll be leaving on Saturday, Molly. But I hardly think a reservation will be necessary. There are usually plenty of seats. I have to be back to my office on Monday, but I wanted to get back in time for church services in Austin on Sunday."

"That's another thing I wished to ask about—"

Elise moved toward Martha, taking her attention from the talking couple.

"—I've searched all over Austin for a church like ours to attend." Molly shamed the truth. "I haven't located the church yet, and I knew Grandmother wouldn't wish me to change churches. Would you be so kind as to give me directions to the sanctuary?"

"It's just a small storefront."

"What's good enough for a man who works at the capitol is good enough for a poor country girl."

"Tell me where you live, and I'll try to direct you."

Molly was caught. She could never bring herself to give Alan the address of her flophouse in the city's questionable quarters. She would lose all chances of winning his affection if she did. So she named a posh boarding-house on one of the popular avenues, and Alan went for a pen to draw her a rough map.

Molly kept Alan occupied until time for the party to begin. Martha gritted her teeth.

Elise flitted about like a beautiful butterfly, touching those about her with cheer, promising the children she would catch fireflies with them after dark.

The evening crept like a snail for Martha as she fought the tightness in her stomach and the dryness in her mouth. She watched Molly while Molly watched Alan.

But no mother ever enjoyed her role more than Nellie as she showed off her children. Her big moment came at the conclusion of the gift opening. She called Susan to her side and whispered something in her ear.

The child held up a hand as would a guard at a railroad crossing and said in a clear, sweet voice, "Thank you. Now my father has something he would like to read."

It was a tribute William had written to their God-given children to climax the welcoming party. With father-ly pride he stood and, like an orator, let the words flow.

"Since eternity, God knew that one day Susan and Billy would be ours. From their births, God had them pick-ed out and especially designed to fill our open hearts and empty arms.

"Most of you know how we waited and waited, some-times almost despairing. God waited, too. He had a special purpose in mind. Down through time, He saw a boy and a girl who would need a home and a home that would need a boy and a girl. It was worth the wait. In our hearts, we know these children have been ours forever.

"What would a journey through life be without tooth fairies and wishes on stars and good-night hugs? God didn't want us to miss out on all that. So He bundled up some sugar and spice in packages of delightful youngsters and sent them by special delivery to our post. We think God hand-picked the most beautiful children just for us. Already, they are the sunshine of our lives.

"We will need each of your prayers, our mothers' advice, and a helping hand now and then as we guide the feet of these little ones in the path of righteousness.

"We want to tell our mothers, friends, neighbors, brothers and sisters, nieces and nephews that we plan to go to heaven as a family."

Martha wished the gilded moment could last forever, frozen in time. But she had learned long ago that moments aren't for keeps; they are for spending. She knew that moments have an expiration date, and like the leftover meat in the Israelites' quail pails, they spoil if hoarded. One must use them or lose them.

There would be future joys, future sorrows, more gains, more losses. But now it was enough to know that Nellie had found her happiness. Almost under the spell of Nellie's rainbow, Martha forgot to worry about Alan's fate.

Almost.

CHAPTER TWENTY FOUR

Martha's Prayer

Chester was the first to leave. His wife called twice more, her indignation swelling with each call. She had put money in escrow to secure the property she wanted for the new hospital. Time was running short for the finalization of the contract. Chester's signature must be on the deed.

Alan took Chester to the train depot, and Susan, whom Nellie accused of becoming a regular chatterbox, begged to go along. She had never seen a train.

At the terminal, Chester reminded Alan to stop by the drug store to pick up some linament for Michael's ankle. "It's still hurting him," he remarked. "It would help if he'd stay off it!"

With grandiloquent newness, the iron horse waited for its few passengers to board. Then it churned up loose dirt from the track and fanned it out as it puffed away with Chester aboard. The fascination of the machine was the rods on the hugh wheels, Alan thought. They moved in the direction opposite the wheels, making the contraption appear to be trying to go two directions at once. Susan waved until the apparition was out of sight, and Alan was glad he could part with Chester with peace in his heart about his twin's spiritual condition.

"Let's go have a soda," Alan suggested to his talkative niece. She was at the age of easily bought delight. While the druggist filled the medicine order, Alan seated Susan and asked what flavor she preferred.

A familiar voice snagged his attention. "Look here!" Molly clicked her long fingernails on the hardwood counter. "My favorite people! Please let me treat you today."

"You didn't tell me you were working here," Alan teased. "This is a surprise. Susan and I were just on our way home from taking Chester to the train station—"

"I just came in this one day for old time's sake. I used to work for Mr. Jacobs, and he was a good employer. He put up with my immaturity and inexperience. Being behind this counter makes me feel like a teenager again, and everybody needs that now and then. You say you brought Chester to the train? Did he have to leave so soon?" She slid the sodas across the counter.

"The parting of the ways has begun, I'm afraid. All good things have to end sometime. Joseph and Amy are heading back for New Mexico in the morning and Dessie and her family about noon. We're trying to stagger the going so that Mama will have a chance to say her farewells properly to each group. She likes it that way. Arthur and Lucy will follow Dessie—"

The door to the business establishment opened, striking the bell on the string.

Molly's attention shifted. She no longer smiled at Alan. A startled look that turned her eyes to flint obsessed

190

her as she gazed beyond him to someone else.

"Molly!"

The man's voice slapped her. She narrowed her eyelids to slits and turned white around the mouth. "What are you doing here, Eli?"

"Why, what do you think, Molly, dear? I'm looking for *you.* Old pennies keep showing up, don't they?"

"*Bad* pennies." She clenched her teeth. "How did you know—"

"Your roommate in Austin, who called herself a demon, told me where I could expect to find you. I should have known. This is where I found you the first time. Right here." He gave a hollow laugh.

Molly's lips quivered in a tormented life of their own. "Eli, you are to leave me alone! I want nothing more to do with you *now* or *ever.*" The words coiled after him like a whip. "If you try to follow me to Granny Myrt's, I'll have you arrested! Do you understand?"

Alan saw that Molly was near to hysteria. She turned to him. "I'm . . . I'm getting terribly sick, Alan. Could . . . could you take me home? Please?" Her voice implored.

"Why, certainly. Hurry with your soda, Susan. Molly is ill and needs a ride along home with us."

The druggist called Alan to the back to get the ointment while Molly and the man carried on a short conversation in low, threatening tones. Molly gestured toward Alan.

Alan helped the young woman into the buggy, supplementing strength for her drooping body with his arm. She sat next to him, rather closely, professing to need support.

The man who had accosted her, Alan noticed, walked

away with a sneer. He stood watching from a safe distance.

Hardly out of town, Molly said she was feeling much better. "That terrible man almost scared me to death," she said. "I hope I shall never see him again!"

"Who was he?" Alan asked.

"He's a man who pursued me years ago when I was scarcely out of my childhood. He had a temporary job in the Springs, and he came to the drugstore so often that Mr. Jacobs had to ask him to leave. But he would hang around outside waiting for me to get off work. I've always been frightened of him. Oh, if only I had a father or a brother to protect me!" Crocodile tears fell onto her collar.

"Don't worry now," soothed Alan. "Try to forget it. We'll be going back to Austin on Saturday, and surely he won't follow you there."

"I should hope not. But you heard him say that he had been there looking for me. And I cannot believe my girlfriend would have revealed my whereabouts to such a character! She wasn't thinking. Oh, Alan, whatever shall I do?"

"Don't cry. We'll think of something."

"The man has some infamous past. I think he may even be a . . . a murderer!" The more she talked, the more she invented. She craved Alan's sympathy, his attention. "Did you see the way he looked at Susan? He . . . he's not safe around women."

"Try to put it out of your mind."

"Please, Alan, you won't let Granny Myrt know anything about today, will you? Or . . or *anybody?* With Granny's heart condition, she would likely die if she knew I was in danger. And if she should die, I'd be left with the complexities of her property to see after. Such a bother! She has everything willed to me. I'm her only living heir. And I'm . . . I'm afraid this evil man knows this."

"I won't mention it."

"And the child? She won't say anything, will she?" She wrapped her arm around Susan in a gesture of mock embrace. "Even if one other person should find out, there might be a slip."

"Susan, you're not to say anything about the man who distressed poor Molly, do you understand? Not to *anyone*. Not even Matilda."

"Yes, Uncle Alan."

The rest of the trip passed pleasantly enough. Susan called their attention to the field of abundant bluebonnets. *She's a wise child,* Alan told himself, *to try to wash away Molly's fears with the purgative of childish prattle.* "Do flowers have such pretty bonnets in Austin, Uncle Alan?"

"Just as lovely, pet. But in the city, the poor blooms are caged up in flower beds. Austin is a big city. A bit crowded for a boy accustomed to the outdoors. But I keep remembering what Papa used to tell me: 'Alan, a body has t' bloom where he's planted.' "

"I'm glad I'm planted right where I am," sighed Susan. "I'm glad the wagon wheel broke down by my new mama and you found us. God made it happen that way, didn't He?"

"Yes, I'm sure He did."

"Maybe my talker would never have been fixed if you hadn't found me."

"God has strange ways."

"Do you go to the river *every* day, Uncle Alan?"

"Y-yes."

In a trice, Molly jerked the subject away from Alan's river rendezvous. "And do you see those red flowers with the tall brown middles, Susan? They are called Indian paintbrushes."

When they passed the Harris homestead, Matilda and Martha were sitting in the porch swing. "Please let me out, Uncle Alan," requested Susan. "Matilda is here to play dolls."

Alan pulled the buggy to a stop by the gate, and Molly gave Martha a too-cheerful wave.

"Tell your Grandma Harris that I'll be back after a while, Susan. I may look in on Granny Myrt for a few minutes. It may be my last chance to visit with her before I go back to Austin. But mind you, not a word about Molly's fright. . . ."

He waited for Susan to reach the gate then popped the reins and they were off at a gallop.

"Tell us about the trip with Uncle Alan," Matilda plagued her.

"The train was too noisy. Too big. Too black. Too blustery. But we had fun at the drugstore. Uncle Alan got me a soda. Really, it was Molly who gave it to me, though."

"Molly didn't go with you. How come she came back with you?"

"She just . . . wanted to."

"What did Alan and Molly talk about on the way home?"

Martha turned on her ears.

"They told me not to tell."

"Fiddlesticks!"

"And I promised. *I* talked about the flowers."

Martha let out a tired breath then began her long wait for Alan to come home from Molly's. Oh, if only Henry were here to share her heart's burden! What had he always said? *A joy shared is doubled. A sorrow shared is halved.*

Oh, Henry! Henry! Why did you leave me with a single son to worry about? she cried into her kerchief.

The clock had just struck midnight when she heard Alan putting the horses in the barn.

She prayed one single prayer: that she could accept Alan's choice of a wife with dignity.

CHAPTER TWENTY FIVE

A Boy or a Man?

"You new here with the railroad?" An old-timer squinted toward Eli Adams as Eli sat with the men on spit-and-whittle corner. A wiry little man with a threadbare scalp, the old-timer laid claim to a voice with a volume twice his size.

"No, I'm just passing through," Eli replied, his mind too preoccupied to either spit or whittle. "Resting a spell before going on. I'm on leave from the telephone company."

What was Molly doing with Mattie's child? Had she found Mattie by some fluke of fate? And had Mattie ratted on him? He thought he had Molly convinced that he had not been married before. And hadn't the windbag in Seminole said that the *Taylors* had come for the children?

He'd known the minute he saw the child in the drugstore that she was the daughter of his ex-wife. Susan was the spirit and image of her mother; she had her mother's

197

eyes. And who was the man with Molly? A twinge of jealousy gouged him.

"Where can I find a room here?" he inquired.

"Frankly, there's nothing to brag on here for rooms. Mrs. Duvall has a few to rent," spoke up the wizened bystander who loved to begin sentences with adverbs. "Frankly, they're too expensive for the service you get. Her house backs on the crick, and you might enjoy crawdad fishing while you rest a spell. But frankly, Mrs. Duvall is no cook. The cafe here serves up a good fare, though." He spat a stream of tobacco juice toward a soup kitchen across the street.

Crawdad fishing, indeed! Eli's plans were to do some spying on Molly. He took the room, closed the door, and began to map out his strategy.

His clue came unexpectedly. Slipping from bush to bush along the road in Brazos Point so as not to be seen, he stopped his movement when Susan and Matilda came to the mailbox directly across from his hiding place.

He was afraid to proceed, afraid they would discover him. And Susan might recognize him as "the awful drugstore man."

The girls stood talking at the post box.

"I wish you could tell me what Molly and Uncle Alan were talking about yesterday on the way home from town," Matilda wheedled. "I wouldn't tell."

"I can't because I promised," answered Susan. "Secrets can't be told."

"Were they making plans?"

"Yes. But don't ask me any more questions. Not even yes-or-no ones because I won't say."

Matilda sighed. "Gran'ma wanted Uncle Alan to get

himself a wife so he wouldn't be a bacher, but she was hoping on someone different than Molly. And so was I."

"I think Molly is nice. She fixed me and Alan a soda. She learned how to fix sodas when she was a middle-aged girl. She'd have made you one too if you had been there. Then you'd see how nice she is. She even put her arm around me on the way home and told me about the Indian-headed flowers."

"Do you ever miss your mother, Susan? I mean, your *real* mother? If my mother died, I'd miss her so no matter who took me."

"Yes, I miss her." Susan was quiet for a moment. "Sometimes I still see her in my dreams. But she told me before she died to try not to cry because she was going to heaven to be with Jesus, and she really wanted to go. She said Jesus would give me a good mommy to take care of me—or I would live with Grandma—until I came where she was. She tried to tell me about the place she was going. It must be a really nice place, and Jesus must be rich. 'Course, I think my new mommy is rich, too."

"I have a little sister in heaven," offered Matilda. "I never saw her, but my mother told me about her. Your mother can take care of her for my mother. They can keep each other company until the rest of us get up there."

"That would be nice—and it would give my mother something to do. She wouldn't like to be idle," reasoned Susan, "or lonesome."

"Anyway, I'm glad you've come to be my cousin."

"Alan says God has strange ways. One reason He sent me here is so Uncle Chester could fix my tongue so I could talk. Can you suppose what it was like not being able to talk like everybody else?"

"Do you miss your brothers?"

"Sometimes yes and sometimes no," Susan said with blatant practicality. "They pulled my hair and hit me sometimes."

"All brothers are like that."

"They were just my part-brothers, you know. I belonged to my mother, Mattie Taylor, before she married, and my name was Taylor, too. The boys, Rufus and Oscar, were last-named Adams, but their paw ran out on them before they got old enough to say his name. My mother cried and cried."

Behind the persimmon bush, Eli squirmed.

"What kind of paw would leave his children? A yellow coward one, I'd say. Cheap as a chipped penny!" Matilda spat the venomous words. "*My* paw would never do a thing like that. Why, he'd—he'd die first!"

"My mama said their paw might be dead."

"A dead paw would be better than a coward paw."

"Mama surely needed help with the boys. They were a handful, 'specially after she took sick. She said all boys need a paw to guide them through life. So she wrote a letter to the place he once worked, but she never got an answer. Then she just got God to help her before she went to live with Him."

"Aren't you glad you and Billy won't ever have to worry about your Papa William running out on you?"

The girls moved back toward the house, taking their conversation with them. But what they had said ate away at the self-esteem of the man behind the shrubbery. He had been branded a coward by a slip of a girl. He repeated the word in a hoarse whisper, and it left a bitter taste in his mouth.

What kind of paw would leave his children?

One of the boys he had not even waited to see. He had not known for years whether the child was a boy or a girl. He had wanted to party, carouse, and be free from the strings of parenthood.

His own father had walked out on him. He still remembered the ache of that betrayal, the feeling of abandonment that would not go away. Had he not been good enough to merit his father's attention? Had he done something to destroy his father's love, to drive him away? He still bore scars left by these unanswered questions from his own childhood. What if his sons felt the same way?

Eli was seldom sober long enough for his conscience to talk to him, but it had caught him by surprise today, and the neglected faculty was unrelenting. *Cheap as a chipped penny . . . cheap as a chipped penny. . . .*

Mattie was gone, and there could be no restitution made for the misery he had caused her. The tears. The struggle. But what of Molly? Would any repentance on his part bring her back to him? According to the girls' conversation, she wasn't married yet, but obviously plans were underway. Was there hope for a reconciliation?

In the drugstore, Molly had been defensive. He couldn't blame her. He had provided her little money and less companionship during their short, turbulent marriage laden with childish embroilments. He was as much to blame as she for the breakup. Maybe more.

What now? He would go back to his room in the Springs, he decided, and write Molly a letter, explaining everything. How he'd had a change of mind and heart. How he'd like to straighten up his life and be a good husband—and father.

With this decision, he stood upright and squared his shoulders. It was never too late for an irresponsible boy to become a man. . . .

Through the leaves he saw a man—the same man in whose company Molly left the drugstore—walking hurriedly from the back of the Harris house toward the river. He might be going fishing, but he had no pole, no worms, no tackle.

Then he saw something else. Something that made flames of red run up his neck to his ears.

He saw Molly slipping through the trees from the opposite direction, careful that no one see her.

So they were meeting clandestinely at the river!

I've lost her! With his fingernails digging into the palms of his hands, he ran back toward Walnut Springs to his shabby room at the boardinghouse.

I've lost her!

CHAPTER TWENTY SIX

A Proposal for Molly

Myrt found the letter anchored to the door with a rusty nail.

"Molly! You have a letter!" she called. Her voice always came out in a cracked little whine.

Molly, supposing the message was from Alan, jumped up to take it from her grandmother's shaking hands.

She ripped open the envelope and was well into the contents of the letter before her mind thought to question the identity of the writer.

Dear Molly,

Please believe me when I say that I've decided that I truly love you and can't go on living without you.

She smiled up at Myrt and said, "Oh, Granny! It must be from my dear, sweet Alan. I knew he would come to the conclusion that he loves me sooner or later." She read the first line aloud to Myrt, her eyes bright with the excitement of it. Myrt mumbled her approval. "And listen, Granny!"

I do have some confessions to make, though, as I want

*to start our new relationship on a basis of honesty. I hope
that you will accept my apologies, find it in your heart
to forgive me, and still consider me a worthy husband after
I have exposed my past.*

Myrt frowned. "Now whatever could Alan Harris be
talking about? He always has been an honest and right-
eous boy! There's not a finer anywhere."

*Maybe you already know what I am about to tell you.
I have had a previous marriage to which were born two
little boys—*

"No!" Myrt's hand fluttered to her throat. "I ven-
ture that not even *Martha* knows that dark secret! And
if she finds out, it'll about kill her. She put so much stock
in Alan."

*—and I hope that together you and I will be able to
take my children and raise them with love and
understanding.*

"Could you do it, Molly? Could you raise Alan's sons
by some other woman without feeling resentful and mean?
Could you love them like your own?"

"I told Alan as much, Grandma. I wondered why he
looked at me so strangely when he was talking about
Nellie adopting those children and I told him that I would
be glad to do the same for some motherless child. I didn't
know he had thoughts of his own children. Oh, I'm glad
now that I said what I did. That's probably what gave
him the courage to make this confession to me, knowing
I'd understand and help him."

*I visited the place in Austin where you live, and I want
you to have better.*

"Granny! I didn't even know Alan knew I was in
Austin before this trip home. He's never mentioned com-

ing by my apartment while I was at work. I guess he must have loved me all along if he has been keeping tabs on me."

She didn't wait for Myrt's comments.

The old life is over, Molly. There's to be no drinking or gambling or running around. It's a promise.

"Did you do all those wicked things, Molly?" interrupted Myrt, her piercing eyes on her granddaughter. "Is he scolding you? What does he mean?"

"Alan probably heard that I did some of those things, Granny. People like to talk about widows who live alone in a city. But you know me better than that. You taught me to be upright and decent. The worst I ever did was work as a soda jerk in Walnut Springs. And what trouble could a body get into in that sleepy town? That rumor-spreading girl that I share a room with is apt to tell anything, and she must have filled Alan's ears with trash. But I'll tell him none of it was true."

We'll want to take the children to church and teach them about the God their mother died believing in.

"She's dead, then," Molly said. "Alan's first wife is dead, Granny. And with me losing Eli, I will know just how to assuage Alan's bouts of grief—"

"I never noticed him saddened."

"Like myself, he's trying to forget the past. He now makes this proposal because he realizes we have so much in common. Each of us losing a companion—oh, can't you see the wisdom of it all, Granny dear? Can't you see how I can comfort him and he can comfort me, and we can both comfort the children? I know I've given you occasion to worry, Granny, and the parson thought me incorrigible, but I had already decided to change my lifestyle.

My marrying Alan meets with your approval, doesn't it?"

"Oh, yes, child. I've always championed Alan. And Martha will bring herself to be accepting of you when she learns that both of you are sorrowing together. Death of Alan's wife will fret Martha less than a divorce. Well, poor, poor Martha. She never knew her now deceased daughter-in-law. She'd have wanted her laid to rest in the family plot. 'Tis hard to imagine Martha not even knowing about it and the Harrises being such a close family. But Alan being away from home so long and so far kept his secret."

I don't know what you were doing with Mattie's child—and I don't know who the man was whom you were with in the drugstore, but—

Here, Molly pulled her brows down until they faced each other like two angry caterpillars. Some light of comprehension burst over the horizon of her illusion.

"What does he mean by that, Molly?" pressed Myrt. "Who is Mattie's child?" But Molly wasn't listening. She had turned to the last page of the letter and had seen Eli's signature at the end. In a rage of pure madness, she flung the pages to the floor.

"The reprobate!" she screamed. "I will not read another word written by his vile hands!"

"Molly! Don't dare say that about one of Martha's—!"

The young woman sobbed in wild gasps. "It's not from Alan. It's from *Eli Adams!*"

"But you told me Eli was *dead!*"

"He was. Or . . . he was supposed to be. I mean . . . I mean, I *wish* he was! As far as I'm concerned, he *is* dead. Any feelings I ever had for the viper are gone. Forever!"

"Something smells fishy, Molly. You'd better finish the letter."

"I will not!"

"Then I shall."

"You shall not."

"Any man deserves the right to be heard clean through to the end, be he devil or be he saint. Can't you see that he's trying to make amends?"

"It's too late for amends."

Myrt bent down to retrieve the letter, but Molly snatched it up. "No!"

"Then *you* read it." The command had the strength of a Myrt in her vigorous fifties. The whine was gone.

I hope I haven't waited too late. Yesterday I saw myself for what I was to walk out on a woman and two helpless children that I had fathered. I was a yellow coward. But I want the chance to prove myself a man.

Please meet me in town tomorrow, Molly darling, so that we may discuss the possibility of a reconciliation.

All my love,

Eli Adams

The old lady sat rocking, thinking her own thoughts while Molly stormed. Gradually, Molly's tirade spent itself and only the raw anger remained.

"He has asked to be forgiven, Molly," Myrt finally said, "and the Bible says we must be willing to forgive seventy times seven. Did you ever figure that up?"

"Did I ever figure what up?"

"That multiplication sum. How many forgivings that would be."

"I don't plan to waste any forgiveness on Eli Adams."

Myrt ignored her. "The Bible is talking about an ongoing forgiveness, Molly. Do you know that forgiveness is the highest form of love?"

Scorn curled Molly's lips. "I don't love Eli Adams in the lowest form, much less the highest!"

"Your vows say cling."

"That's an outdated idea, Grandma."

"You won't even talk to him?"

"I won't. There's no use. He had his chance, and he left me. Now I am in love with another man."

"You're talking about Alan Harris?"

"No other. I plan to marry Alan. We will be going back to Austin on Saturday, and I will get him. Just you wait and see. I *will* be Mrs. Alan Harris. I will not let that girl in Austin have him!"

"What girl?"

"Never mind."

"Does Alan know about Eli?"

"He doesn't. Eli came into the drugstore while I was treating Alan and his niece to a soda. I told Alan he was a man I had once met and I wanted nothing more to do with him. Alan brought me directly home."

"I think you should tell Alan about your previous marriage."

"I'll tell him in my own time. Please stay out of it."

"Why would someone have sent word that Eli was dead if he wasn't?"

"There are mixups all the time at the telephone company, Granny. I'm sure there's more than one Eli Adams in the world."

"Martha Harris thinks Eli is dead."

"And she must not learn that he isn't. It might ruin my plans."

"Yes, I'm afraid Martha would object to her son marrying someone who already has a husband."

"I have no husband."

"What if Eli shows up?"

"He won't. I threatened him and put the fear of God in him. And in just a few more hours, I will be leaving. . . ."

"You don't suppose Eli will follow you to Austin?"

"I will already be married to Alan by the time he shows up. Leave it to me, Granny. I know how to play the game."

"Molly! Molly!" Myrt shook her white head and gave her granddaughter a pitying look. "It's a mighty dangerous game you're playing."

CHAPTER TWENTY SEVEN

Not a Single Worry

"Look what I found, Uncle Alan."

Alan put the last of his clothing into his portmanteau and raised his eyes to Michael, who held a pocket knife in his open hand.

"It has a name inscribed on it: E. Adams."

"Where did you find it?"

"Behind the persimmon bush across the road from Grandmama's."

"It's a nice knife. I don't know anyone by that name. Wait—I've heard that name somewhere. Wasn't that the last name of the little boys with the Taylors? Adams. Yes, I believe it was. One of them must have dropped it. I wouldn't know how to get it back to them, though. It was some little boy's treasure. . . ."

Alan went back to his packing. He hated the thought of going back to the churning city. His time spent in the country had been a time of solace and contrast. He felt renewed in spirit and mind. He'd been with those he loved, and the worry of Chester's soul was behind him.

He had benefited especially from the family's annual memorial at the graveyard. There had been thirty-three of them in all. His family. Only Nellie and Chester's wife were missing. Nellie stayed in with little Billy.

The morning, sun-soaked and tranquil, had seemed custom ordered for the day of sentiments. Martha, marinating in memory's sweet essence, looked up and remarked to Alan, "The sky's a nice place to look, but I'm notioned it'll be a better place to be."

They took flowers and wreaths to place on the graves then joined hands around the mounds of Henry, little Robert, and Sarah's baby. Martha said Henry seemed "jest in th' other room." With one hand Alan held his mother's and with the other, Sally's. Matthew offered a prayer of thanksgiving for the lives of those deceased and a petition for those yet alive in the family circle.

Each shared memories of special moments with their departed loved ones, mingling laughter and tears. There were hugs and kisses and promises to be back the next year.

Two wagons were needed to take the family into town to see Alan's train off. Feeble Myrt, looking suddenly older, insisted on going to see Molly safely deposited. Martha, determined to the end to protect her grown son, again arranged the seating so that Alan took his place with the men and Molly with the women.

Hank wedged the adults in the big wagon, and William offered to bring the children along in the smaller. Michael, his ankle still weak, dawdled so that it was necessary for the departing travelers to go on in order to get their tickets. "We'll make it in time," William promised. "The old huffer-puffer is always late."

Sitting in the back with Myrt, Martha found herself subjected to Molly's verbiage.

"I can hardly wait to be back in Austin," she clucked. "Alan has promised to take me to his church and introduce me to his friends." Molly, with most of her rouge and eye paint missing, looked a bit lost. *She has changed,* Martha admitted to herself, *but not enough.*

"But Molly, what about—?"

"Granny, please don't try to talk!" Molly demanded. "The wind will give you a sore throat, and I won't be here to nurse you. Save your voice for the goodbyes." She put her hand over the old lady's toothless mouth.

"Molly, I think you should tell Martha—"

Molly pinched her. "You'll be ill, Granny."

"I know that you'll be glad, Mrs. Harris, to have someone to look after Alan in that big place." Molly's voice was syrupy. "It's not good for a man to be alone there. There are too many temptations."

"I trust Alan," retorted Martha.

"Oh, surely, but we don't trust the wild women." She laughed. "Granny gave me some of her best recipes, and I'm going to learn to cook especially for Alan. Could you tell me what he likes best? I want, more than anything, to please him."

Martha swallowed hard, tried to think back to the night Alan talked on her horn. Hadn't he said, "We'll want a place of our own"? A horrible thought attacked her. He wasn't talking about the girl in Austin; he was talking about himself and Molly!

"What did you ask?"

"What foods does Alan like?"

Looking back, Martha never knew why she did it, but

213

some perverse idea came to her mind to name all the things Alan couldn't stand! Granted, it wasn't the Christian thing to do, and she knew she would have to apologize to Molly, but just now she derived a vengeful delight from the farce.

She began her enumeration. "Oh, he likes tripe an' hogshead cheese an' clabber an' jowl. Make all his cakes without eggs an' leave th' saleratus an' th' salt out of his flapjacks. Men are particular. That boy was my most picayunish eater."

"I hope I can remember all that," fretted Molly.

"Alan'll remind you if you mistake," Martha said woodenly.

"Well, I'm surprised he et anything I cooked," mused Myrt, "with an appetite as crotchety as that."

The second wagon ran about a half hour behind but with plenty of time for the departure. It was filled with rowdy good humor. Susan talked almost nonstop. "The front of the train looks like it has big teeth, doesn't it?"

"That's a cowcatcher," Michael said. He had long cherished an ambition to be an engineer and considered himself an authority on trains.

"And a man with a funny hat rides in the red car on the back."

"He's the brakeman," supplied Michael, "and the last car is the caboose."

"He runs alongside the train and jumps on. I hope he never misses."

"He won't. That's what he's trained to do."

"There's two big square things on the front."

"Lanterns."

"Do trains have names?"

"Yes," Michael said. "One of the first trains was named Tom Thumb. Another was Old Ironsides. Alan's train is called the Doodlebug."

The station was abustle when they arrived; several passengers stood at the ticket window. Molly stood right at Alan's elbow as they waited their turn in line. Running her fingers across her lips, she shot her grandmother a warning look.

Eli Adams heard the distant whistle of the locomotive and slipped across the creek to the back of the depot, keeping out of sight. He yearned for one more glimpse of Molly before she left. He had concluded that since she had not met him in town, she would never concede to be reunited with him. This was probably the last time he would ever see her, he decided, and the thought made him miserable. Sometimes one waited too late to turn around, and that's what had happened with Molly. However, he had pledged to himself that he would become a real man with or without her. Wherever they were, he would find his sons, and if he had to rear them alone, well, so be it.

The train came to a hissing halt, heaving out its last black breath and shaking its internal organs all the way to its caboose. A few passengers got off, but most were getting on.

Alan stepped to a small porch and looked over his beloved family. He held up his hand for their attention.

"I have an announcement to make," he grinned. "And a confession, too, which may account for the fact that I never caught any fish! The truth is I *wasn't* fishing. I planned to, but something more important took my time. I was sparking a beautiful young lady all those hours on the creek bank—"

Martha sucked in her breath and looked as though she might cry. She wanted to stop her ears, to turn and run so that she would not have to hear the rest of what Alan had to say. She was afraid. Afraid of how she would react or what she would say. Afraid she would show her bitter disappointment.

"We are very much in love and plan to be married in just a few weeks."

Molly moved through the crowd with a smile of ecstasy to stand beside Alan.

"I hope that all my family will love my bride-to-be as dearly as I do."

I can't! Martha's heart cried. *Oh, God, I can't. Alan, please don't expect this of me. Henry . . . Henry . . . .*

"If my betrothed will join me, I want you all to meet her. . . ."

Nobody had noticed the serene woman moving quickly from the back of the press toward Alan, never taking her adoring eyes from him. She had gotten off the second wagon.

"Gra'ma, she has on the same dress she had on at the river!" Matilda whispered, pulling at Martha's sleeve.

Martha looked toward Molly, giving attention for the first time to what she was wearing. Her dress was not checked at all.

"Shhh, Matilda. Alan's announcin'."

Elise Young, blushing and radiant, took his out-stretched hand as he lifted her to the short podium. Alan bowed, kissed her hand.

"Ladies and gentlemen! The future Mrs. Alan Harris!"

Elise curtsied.

"But Tilly," Martha said, somewhat incoherently,

"you said *red* plaid, and Miss Young's dress is *blue.*" Happy tears left pools in her eyes.

"I never said no color, Gra'ma. You didn't ask me."

The family moved in to congratulate Elise and Alan. All eyes were on them except Michael's. His enthrallment with the seething engine was complete.

"I got the appointment at Brazos Point for my Elise, but I just loaned her to you for the rest of the school term," Alan said. "When school is out for the summer, she's all mine!"

"Alan! How did you keep your secret so . . . so perfectly?" Sally asked. "There wasn't a hint!"

"From the minute I arrived, I knew my family's wishes—and intentions. I overheard the plans to find me a wife. And since they coincided so precisely with my own, Elise and I decided to surprise all of you with our last-minute proclamation. Selfish we were, but we wanted our short time together to be alone. You'll have to forgive me—as you always do. . . ." He blew them a kiss. "To the best family in the world: Long live the house of Harris!"

Unseen by any save Myrt, Molly stepped down from the platform into the waiting arms of Eli Adams. He smoothed her raven hair and held her as she laid her head on his shoulder and wrapped her arms about him. "There, there, Molly!" he crooned. "Don't cry, precious. You belong to me, and I'll make everything right. Here, let me get your suitcase, and you'll come with me. . . ."

Myrt's face was bathed in relief, and a lopsided smile straightened out part of her wrinkles. Molly's game was over.

"Aunt Sally—" Matilda tugged at Sally's sash, "Gra'ma won't have a worry now, will she?"

A *Single Worry*

"No." Sally looked at Martha, seeing motherly pride written in the smile she gave her son. *"Not a single worry."*